'It was about page three of *2000f*  burst inside me: the joy of recognis complicated . . . Everything on the pa I've read before.' —Alie Benge, *The Spi*

'*2000ft Above Worry Level* is a real sign of the times. It is polite, non-assertive and devastating. Marra's tone is simple and declarative, but his content reveals a world where you don't want to laugh, but you do because the only other option is to cry – and you don't want to do that.' —David Herkt, *Stuff*

'Even when the subjects are depression, alienation and anhedonia, the good, focused and tone-perfect prose and the understated humour collaborate to make *2000ft Above Worry Level* more than an impressive debut . . . It's cunning. It gradually builds up a totally credible picture of a complex human being. It is everything it should be.' —Nicholas Reid, *Landfall Review Online*

'An episodic series of connected pieces, this novel is written in a spare, laconic style and deals with anxiety, depression, awkward cam sex, and unemployment – but with the most brilliant sense of comic timing and a lightness of touch. It's remarkably laugh-out-loud funny and touching, too.' —Kiran Dass, *95bfm*

'Each sentence is like a dropped rock in your chest. It's really, really funny and also it can absolutely destroy you, cos you're rolling along with his casual bluntness and then he uses the same casual bluntness to drop in some devastating detail . . . He doesn't make any excuses for his protagonist, who does some interesting untangling of some fucked-up attitudes – Eamonn approaches that with tenderness but without pulling punches. My absolute favourite character is the mum. Ugh, I love her.' —Freya Daly Sadgrove, *Starling Magazine*

2000ft ABOVE WORRY LEVEL

EAMONN MARRA

Victoria University of Wellington Press

VICTORIA UNIVERSITY OF
WELLINGTON
TE HERENGA WAKA

Victoria University of Wellington Press
PO Box 600, Wellington
New Zealand
vup.wgtn.ac.nz

Copyright © Eamonn Marra 2020
First published 2020
Reprinted 2021

A catalogue record is available at the National Library of New Zealand

ISBN 9781776562978

Published with the assistance of a grant from

ARTS COUNCIL OF NEW ZEALAND *TOI AOTEAROA*

Printed by BlueStar, Wellington

For my friends

CONTENTS

1

DOG FARM, FOOD GAME

I used to spend a lot of time on the sad part of the internet. Most people don't realise there is a sad part of the internet. Some people think the whole internet is sad and that only sad people spend all their time on the internet. They're wrong – while sad people do spend a lot of time on the internet, it isn't a prerequisite. The sad part of the internet is a special place that only sad people can access. It's full of content made by sad people for sad people. Jokes that make sad people laugh, but would make not-sad people worried. Photos of people crying, but sexy. Mundane descriptions of household objects and everyday activities made special by the knowledge that whoever wrote it felt absolutely terrible at the time. It's easy to fall in love on the sad part of the internet. You have an instant connection because you share the same feeling at all times: sadness. First, you favourite each other's depression jokes, then you message casually, then obsessively, and then you have cam sex.

The first time I had cam sex with Abby it was fast and silent. We didn't want to speak out loud to each other, in case anyone in our homes overheard. We turned on our webcams, and soon her top was off and I typed 'wow' on my keyboard. I pulled my pants down around my knees and got my cock out of my underwear. I tried to find a position for my laptop where my cam would show both my cock and my face, but I couldn't make the angles work.

'Do you want to see my cock or my face?' I typed.

'Are you going to feel bad about whatever I don't say?' she typed back.

'No.'

'Cock then.'

I tipped my laptop screen forward to focus on that, then further forward again so my chest wouldn't be in shot. 'Can I see your . . .' I said.

'No, not today,' she said.

She played with her nipples and put her fingers in her mouth, then it was over and I came into my hand and I showed her my handful of cum.

'Was that good for you?' I asked.

'Yeah. It was great,' she said.

I went and got myself cleaned up, and when I got back to the computer she was still there. She was still beautiful after I came. She had put her clothes back on and was sitting in a pile of messy sheets, waiting for me.

'You're beautiful,' I said.

'I am not,' she said.

'You are honestly one of the prettiest girls I've ever met,' I said.

'You're just saying that because I made you come,' she said.

'I am not,' I said. 'Girls as pretty as you don't usually like guys like me.'

'What are you talking about,' she said. 'You're like a big handsome dog. I'm a hairless cat.'

12

'Let's agree to disagree,' I said.

She looked at the camera and tipped her head to the side, like she was trying to get water out of her ear. I smiled. She poked her tongue out at me.

'I've been reading,' she said. 'To make someone like you, you're meant to tell them a secret the first day you meet them.'

'What if I already like you?' I said.

'It doesn't matter,' she said. 'We should do it anyway to make sure we keep liking each other. Just in case.'

'Okay,' I said. 'What's your secret?'

'You first,' she said.

'Why?'

'Because I know you already like me.'

'Okay. I have to think.'

'Take your time,' she said. As I was thinking, she sent me a photo of her lying on the ground, covered in puppies. Six little brown ones with big floppy ears. She was pushing one away who was determined to lick her face. She was laughing and looked so good.

'Cute,' I said.

'Thanks,' she said. 'It's the photo I send when I want to impress someone.'

'Where did you get all those puppies?'

'My parents breed them,' she said. 'But in a good way. It's not a puppy mill.'

'That is really cool. Are there any puppies around now?'

'No, we got rid of them all. We've got seven dogs though. Three breeding pairs and my one.'

'Okay, I've thought of one,' I said. 'I'll type it out in one go, so it might take a while.'

As I typed, I noticed her eyes moving around and back and forward. I realised she had minimised the chat window and was checking other websites.

'Here it comes,' I said. 'I went to an all-boys high school, and when I was sixteen it had been three or four years since I had really talked with a girl. So when I started going to parties, there would be these girls there and everyone was acting like it was no big deal. And eventually everyone would get drunk and then people would start making out, and I wanted to be the one to make out with a girl but I had no idea how to do it. I didn't even talk to them, so I'd hover around the people kissing because I thought maybe she would stop kissing whoever she was kissing and start kissing the next closest guy, which was me. It was like I was queueing up for a pash.'

I watched her as she read it. I was hoping she would smile or at least look directly into the webcam, which is as close as we could get to eye contact, but she didn't. It was like she had forgotten she was being watched. It took minutes for her to respond. It felt like she had read it at least twice but finally she responded. 'Did it work?'

'No, of course not.'

'Is that really a secret?' she asked.

'Yeah – well, I've never told anyone that before.'

'You should. It's cute and funny.'

I sent her a picture of me at sixteen. I had hair down past my shoulders, which I hadn't learned to brush, and an oily face that I hadn't learned to wash. I was wearing an oversized suit jacket over the top of a Ramones T-shirt, because I hadn't learned how to dress. 'Would you have kissed this?' I asked.

'Probably. I kissed almost anything,' she said.

'Thanks.'

'When did you have your first kiss?' she asked.

'Only like a year ago. A year and a half ago.'

'Really?'

'Well. My first real proper kiss. I had like a few meaningless kisses before then.' That was a lie. I hadn't had any meaningless kisses. Every kiss I had ever received I had savoured.

'Cute.'

'What about you?'

'I don't remember. When I was fourteen or fifteen I'd get drunk at parties and kiss everyone. I would have kissed you if you were lining up for it.'

'Damn. I was queueing in the wrong place then.'

'Maybe.'

'What's your secret?'

'I don't think I had one. I was just available.'

'No, your secret for me.'

Three flashing dots appeared on the screen that showed she was typing. Then they disappeared. 'Can I let you know tomorrow?' she said.

'That's not how it works. You have to tell someone the first day you meet.'

'But you already like me,' she said. 'I'll tell you tomorrow.'

I let her get away with it, because it was the first time tomorrow had been mentioned. It was a promise that this was going to keep going, and that was more important than a secret.

That night, after eleven hours of talking, we recorded a video of ourselves brushing our teeth. We were both exhausted and desperately needed to sleep, but we felt like we had to commemorate this day with something special. We each set a timer for two and a half minutes. I brushed with my right hand, and held my phone to my chest with my left hand to record my reflection in the mirror. She was left-handed, so she did the opposite. She sent me her video and I edited the videos together side by side. I wore a green T-shirt that was the same colour as her bathroom wall. She wore a red jersey that was the same colour as my bathroom wall. It was unintentional, but felt like a sign. Some sort of aesthetic connection. It ended with us spitting into the sink at exactly the same time. I smiled through my bleeding gums, which matched my walls and her jersey.

I uploaded the video to YouTube and marked it as unlisted so no one could find it by searching and then I sent her the link. I never watched it on YouTube, only ever from the file on my computer, so I could check the play count and see how many times she had watched it, assuming she never sent it to anyone else. By the next day it had been played seven times.

Before I met Abby, I had a coping strategy to get through the days. I would wake up sometime between 11am and 2pm and lie in bed thinking of all the things I needed to do to get my life in order, which would all stack up on top of my chest and it would feel like I was anchored to my bed until I managed to push them all off, promising myself I would deal with them the next day. I would make my way to the lounge, where I would binge-watch a TV series on the television. It had to be something with long episodes and eight or nine seasons, so that it would feel like it went on forever and once I finally finished watching them all it would feel like an achievement. While watching the TV show I would play a game on my phone. It had to be something mindless but that required concentration. The type of game where you have to match coloured gems to make them disappear. And while I was doing that I would browse the sad part of the internet on my computer. My attention would be so spread out that I wouldn't have the time or ability to actually think. Because when I started to think, I had dangerous thoughts. I would do these three things every day for as long as I possibly could, staying up as late as possible so I would fall asleep as soon as I was in bed, because if I was alone in bed without distractions I would have dangerous thoughts. I hadn't answered my phone in a month. I hadn't checked my emails in a month. I hadn't gone to university in a month. I was going to keep doing this until things made sense again. Which they did, when I met Abby.

With her in America and me in New Zealand, we came to a problem. We were only awake at the same time for a small part of every day. So we came up with a solution. We developed our own time zone, one where we would never have to be awake without each other. It worked for both of us because I didn't think my flatmates would notice if I disappeared, and Abby's family left her alone. She didn't eat with them because she had a special diet that completely baffled her parents. We set the clocks on our computers to our time zone. Our 9am was 7pm in New Zealand and 3am in America. We would talk for thirteen hours every day, until our 10pm, which was 8am in New Zealand and 4pm in America. That gave us eleven hours to sleep and do anything else we needed to get done. Every morning I would wake up at 8am (our time), try to look as good as possible for her, and check the count on the teeth-brushing video. By the end of the first week it already had over thirty views.

After a week of our new time zone, my flatmate knocked on my door. 'We haven't seen you for a week,' she said. 'Is everything okay?'

'Things are good,' I said. 'I've just got a fucked-up sleep schedule right now.' And things were good. Abby was good for me. Before Abby, I would spend all day lying on the couch. Abby made me want to sit up, because I looked ugly lying down and I wanted to look good for her. She made me want to change my clothes every day. With her I actually talked to another person. My world opened up, even if it was just a little bit, but it felt like it was the beginning of something important.

We tried talking aloud once. It was midway through the second week. We whispered into our laptops so no one else could hear us and it was weird. We had to get right up close to the computers, and the webcams picked up our acne, which had been a blur until then. We both hated our voices, and talking caused too much anxiety to be worth it. She said she sounded like a little kid because her voice went up and down as if she was half-singing. I had the opposite problem. I could only talk in a monotone and would always sound bored. If I tried to add inflection or enthusiasm I would be overwhelmed with embarrassment.

So other than that one day, the only time I heard Abby's voice was when she talked to her dog Daisy. Daisy was the only dog that I saw, because she was the only one who was allowed in Abby's room. She knew how to get into Abby's room by herself – she stood up on her hind legs, pushed the handle down and leaned on the door to open it.

'Come here Daisy,' Abby would say in her singsong voice whenever Daisy opened the door. Daisy would sit right on top of Abby and put her head on Abby's shoulders. Whenever Daisy sat on Abby, Abby had to pull the computer closer to her and type with one hand. It made the conversation slower and it was harder to see Abby, but I tried not to hold it against Daisy.

'You're a good girl, aren't you Daisy,' Abby said. Daisy wasn't a breeding dog like the others, and she was Abby's responsibility. Abby got Daisy when she was a kid, so she was now getting old. She had grey hair around her mouth and couldn't jump all the way up to Abby's bed anymore. When she wanted to get up she'd put her front paws on the bed, and Abby would lean over and pull her up by her armpits.

'When we got her, her name was Gretchen. So that had to change because Gretchen is a terrible name, and since she was mine I got to choose, and I was a kid so I called her Daisy.'

'Do you not like the name Daisy anymore?'

'It's fine. It's just, of course a ten-year-old would call a dog Daisy. It's better than what Dad would have called her. He called the last dog we got Charisma. That's a stupid name.'

We only turned off our webcams once a day, at 5pm (our time), because Abby didn't want to eat in front of me. I ate baked beans on toast every day because they were fast and cheap. Before I went into the kitchen, I listened at the door so I could avoid my flatmates. I poured a can of baked beans into a big bowl and put it in the microwave for four minutes on high. Some of the beans at the top of the bowl exploded and stuck to the roof of the microwave, and I wiped them off with a paper towel. I ate the beans with four pieces of toast. The beans at the bottom of the bowl would always be cold. Once a week I went to the supermarket and bought seven cans of beans and three loaves of bread. I only ate once a day.

'You never told me your secret,' I said one night after our food break.

'I didn't have to,' she said. 'You already liked me.'

'That's not fair,' I said.

'I never came up with a secret because I didn't know we would keep talking.'

'Were you not going to keep talking to me?'

'Probably not. I usually don't with guys online for long.'

'Oh,' I said.

'Do you usually keep talking to girls you meet online after you have cam sex?'

'No,' I said.

'So why did you keep talking to me?'

'It felt different.'

'Yeah, it did. I guess your secret worked on me.'

'I'm glad it did,' I said.

'I lied to you,' she said. 'I've been feeling bad about it. I told you that I used to kiss lots of people, but I didn't. I didn't go to any parties when I was fourteen or fifteen or sixteen or seventeen. I only kissed someone for the first time earlier this year.'

'Why did you do that?'

'I thought it would be nice for you to have someone you have always wanted.'

'But I didn't know what I wanted. I just wanted someone. Anyone would do.'

'Do you still feel like that?'

'No. I want just one specific person now.'

She smiled. 'Who's that?'

'You wouldn't know her,' I said.

'Do you want this?' she said, and undid a button of her shirt and pulled it open. She traced her fingers around her collarbones.

'Yes please,' I said.

She pushed her computer to the end of the bed and leaned back against her headboard so I could see her whole body. She tilted her head back so her neck lengthened and she pushed her hands through her hair, pulling it off her face. She put her knees up and spread them apart. She put her hand on top of her underwear and rubbed.

'Wow,' I said. Which is what I said every time we started having cam sex.

She pulled her arms inside her shirt and fumbled around,

then took her bra out of one of her sleeves.

I pushed my laptop on an angle so she could see my cock throbbing inside my underwear.

She leaned forward and I saw her breasts inside her shirt as she typed on her computer. 'I want to see your body,' she said.

I pushed my laptop to the edge of the bed. I positioned myself so my neck was up and my stomach was sucked in.

She undid another button on her shirt and pulled one side down to reveal her naked shoulder. She leaned forward again.

'Love that view,' I said.

'Take your T-shirt off,' she said. I hadn't done that before.

I took it off slowly, which I hoped came across as sexy rather than self-conscious. I was bloated from the beans; I tried to pull my stomach in and I made sure I was facing the camera exactly front-on so that she couldn't see my body's depth. 'Mmmm,' she said, undoing another button. She slowly pulled her shirt to the side, to the edge of her nipple. I pulled my cock out of my underwear and let go of it, showing it standing up firm. The door creaked and she pulled her shirt back together, jumped forward and slammed her laptop shut.

I put my T-shirt back on and put my cock back in my underwear and tried to stop touching myself.

A minute later she called me again and I answered. 'It was just Daisy,' she said. She was sitting cross-legged in front of the computer. 'Where were we . . .' She opened her shirt quickly and I got a glimpse of her breast. Then she closed it again.

'Wow.' I pulled my T-shirt back off and pushed my laptop back to the edge of the bed.

She moved against the headboard and pushed the laptop to the other end of the bed so I could see her whole body again. Daisy was there with her front paws on the bed, next to Abby, waiting to be lifted up. 'Not now Daisy,' Abby said, and pushed Daisy down off the bed with a foot.

I touched myself through my underwear. Daisy's tail wagged in and out of the corner of the screen. I leaned forward and tried to not let my fat hang as I typed on the computer. 'Sorry, Daisy is distracting me,' I said.

'Just ignore her,' she said. 'She won't tell anyone.' She sat back down and put her hand inside her underwear. Daisy put her front paws back on the side of the bed. Abby sighed and grabbed Daisy's legs and put her on the ground.

'Can you get her out of your room?'

'She knows how to get back in. She'll just open the door again.'

'Can't you put something against the door?'

'She'll just pine outside the door and that will attract everyone else.'

'I don't know what to do then,' I said. 'I just can't. It's weird.'

'There are dogs everywhere here. If you like me, you have to get used to the dogs.' She pulled her shoulder back into her shirt and buttoned it all the way up to the top button. Daisy put her feet up on the side of the bed and Abby leaned over and pulled her up onto the bed.

We stayed on webcam but didn't talk for the next few hours. Occasionally we would send a link to a funny picture and then smile meekly into the camera. The other person would look at it and chuckle quietly. It was like we were saying, 'I'm not annoyed at you, I just don't know what to say.'

Abby eventually said, 'I need to sleep. Talk to you tomorrow?'

'Yes,' I said. It was an hour and a half earlier than we usually stopped talking.

The next morning (our time) I got up and saw she wasn't

online. I checked the video view count, and for the first time it hadn't gone up since the night before. I got up from my computer and went to the bathroom, where I took off my shirt and pinched myself in my stomach and on my arms and chest. I grabbed handfuls of fat and tried to squeeze them away. I threw water on my face and wiped it off with my towel. When I got back to my computer, she was online. I tried to call her but she rejected the call.

'Sorry, I'm about to eat,' she said.

'What are you eating?' I asked.

'Toast.'

'If I went and made some toast now, could we eat together?'

Dots appeared to show she was typing. Then they disappeared. Then she said, 'Okay.'

I rushed into the kitchen. One of my flatmates was in there. 'Well, well, well,' she said. 'You're alive.'

'Yeah,' I said. 'I'm okay.' I threw four pieces of bread into the toaster and set it to two so it would be done fast.

'What have you been doing?' she asked.

'You know, just depression stuff,' I said. She looked concerned. 'I'm kidding,' I said. 'I've been working on something. Something for uni. I'm catching back up. I'm actually quite happy right now.'

'Good. We're here, y'know. If you want to talk or just hang out. We aren't strangers.'

The toast popped. It was warm but not brown at all and still soft to the touch. I put big lumps of peanut butter on each piece, then tried to spread it. The bread ripped in several places. 'I've got to go,' I said, and took the plate into my room.

I ran back to my laptop and called Abby again. She answered this time. She was sitting cross-legged on her bed. In front of her there was a small plate with a single piece of toast, thinly but evenly spread with jam.

'Have you already started?' I asked.

'No. I don't eat much,' she said.

I felt ashamed of my four pieces of warm bread, thick with lumps of peanut butter.

'Okay, should we eat then?' she said.

'Yeah, okay.'

She nibbled on her toast. Chewing dozens of times for each small bite. I folded my bread in half and took big bites. I swallowed without much chewing. I could eat a piece of bread in two and a half bites. I finished my four pieces before she had finished her one. We didn't talk while eating. But we did look at each other a lot.

'That was weird,' she said.

'I liked it,' I said. 'Can we do this again?'

'Yeah,' she said. 'I miss you when we eat.' She put her plate on the table next to her bed.

Abby and I ate twice a day. We had to decide what we were going to eat that we could both easily get.

'Eggs on toast?' I suggested.

'I've already told you,' she said, 'I'm vegan.'

'I'm basically vegetarian,' I said. I had never made a decision to go vegetarian, I'd just stopped eating meat when I moved out of home because I didn't know how to cook it and I couldn't afford it.

'That's not how it works,' she said. 'You're either vegetarian or not.'

'I am vegetarian,' I said. 'It's been months since I ate meat.' It was mostly true. I had only eaten baked beans for the last few months so I hadn't eaten meat, except for the one time I accidentally bought the baked beans that have tiny sausages in them. 'I just haven't felt the need to label myself.'

We settled on peanut butter on toast. I tried to spread it thin, but it always looked thick compared to hers.

'Sorry about yesterday,' I said a few hours later.

'No, it's okay. It's just Daisy is really special to me. It's a bit of a sore spot.'

'It's also I get a bit uncomfortable about my body,' I said.

'You shouldn't feel bad. I like your body,' she said. 'My dad has always been really mean to Daisy.'

'I've always blamed my body for everything bad that's ever happened to me. Like I would be happier and people would like me more and girls would like me more if I was skinnier.'

'You're a big handsome dog,' she said. 'I bet lots of girls like you.'

'I think I use it as an excuse. Like if no one could possibly like my body, what's the point of even putting myself out there?'

'My dad doesn't like her because she can't have pups,' Abby said.

'And I do this thing, if I like I girl so much I can't hide it, I always frame it as an apology. I say, I'm sorry I like you.'

'Do you like me?'

'Yes.'

'Do you like Daisy?'

'Yes.'

'Great, now you've told two girls you like them.'

'I think I'm going to start doing exercise,' I said. 'I need to get in shape. My doctor keeps telling me exercise will make me feel better. I'll go for a walk later on today.'

'Did you know walking isn't really exercise?' she said. 'It doesn't get your heart rate to the cardio level you need in order to lose weight. It's pretty much worthless.'

'I'll walk up a hill,' I said.

'In fact, walking is worse than worthless, because after you trick yourself into thinking you did exercise when you actually didn't, you treat yourself, and you end up eating more calories than you burned off.'

'I'll power walk up the hill.'

'I run every day.'

'What? When?'

'Straight after we finish talking. I go for half an hour then go to sleep.'

'Every single day?'

'Yes. I take Daisy. If I'm making sure Daisy is fed and exercises every day, then my parents leave me alone. They think I'm okay.'

'You've never told me that,' I said.

'You never asked,' she said.

'I'll go then too, and I'll run, so we are running at the same time.'

'The best way to deal with weight is dieting,' she said. 'It's easier to not let the calories in in the first place than it is to burn them.'

'Yeah, I'm trying to eat less,' I said.

'Sorry,' she said. 'I shouldn't have said that.'

'No, I want to,' I said. 'Maybe we could help each other?'

That evening (our time), I went for a run for the first time in my life. I could only run for about a minute before my legs felt heavy like I could barely lift them off the ground. So I walked for two or three minutes to catch my breath, and then ran again, slower this time. I ran for about three minutes the second time but then my breathing started feeling sharp and like my lungs were only half inflating so I stopped and stretched. I only remembered two stretches from PE class at school so I did both of them over and over again until I was okay to run again. I considered turning around and going home, but the thought of Abby running at the same time made me continue. Other runners on their morning run went past me and they all looked at me. They smiled, which could have been pity, but also could have been encouragement. They were running so much faster than I could and they would disappear into the distance in seconds. I watched their calves as they ran away, they were so toned with large bulges at the top thinning down to tiny ankles. My calves had never looked anything like that. I was not sure whether it was because I'd never tried running or if it was because the other runners were built differently. I had to keep wiping sweat off my forehead with my arm before it reached my eyes and stung.

I got home and looked in the mirror. My T-shirt had big dark patches of sweat around the collar, big enough to reach most of the way down my chest and around my belly button, with a sweat bridge connecting the two patches. My armpits were not as sweaty as I expected, but when I smelled them they smelled bad.

After I had a shower I wiped down the mirror and looked into it for a whole minute, trying to burn what I looked like to memory because it would change soon.

I couldn't sleep because there was so much energy pulsing around my legs, so I went for a small walk around the block and before I knew it, I was in a dairy, buying an ice cream. I had one bite then threw it in the bin. Abby and I had made a promise to only ever eat with each other and I had already broken it. What a waste of $4.50.

Abby and I had an unspoken competition over who could eat the slowest. We sat in silence, cross-legged, staring at our webcams, with our plates in our laps. I took small bites and counted my chews: thirty for each bite. By the thirtieth chew, the toast had completely disintegrated and I was chewing saliva, then I'd swallow. Somehow she still always won.

'Sorry I'm such a slow eater,' she said at our next meal. She didn't have to be sorry. After I was done, I got to watch her and she looked beautiful when she was eating. Every time she chewed it was with conviction. Between bites she licked her lips, searching for any remaining peanut butter. After she was done, she licked the crumbs off her fingers.

I stood up and took my plate to a table across the room. I did this so my crotch would be in shot and Abby would see that I had an erection without it looking intentional. She either didn't notice it or ignored it, so we didn't have cam sex that day.

'Did your parents ever do things that messed you up, but they never really knew?' Abby asked when I got back to my bed. 'Like things that hurt you real bad and they never realised how much?'

'Yeah, definitely,' I said. 'I've been thinking about this for a while. When I was a little kid, I really wanted a desk. Because my parents got my brother a desk when he started school, when he was five, so I would have been three and I wanted one too.'

'My one is about Daisy,' Abby said. 'We actually originally got Daisy as a breeding dog. We got her all the way from Canada, to widen the gene pool.'

'But isn't Canada right there?' I said.

'Yeah, but it's a whole other country. We had to do paperwork and everything.'

'Anyway Mum told me, "You don't need a desk, you've got this coffee table,"' I said.

'But what happened was, she was only two or three, and we

organised a breeding partner for her. And she got pregnant, and when the puppies were born they were completely white with red eyes.'

'Because she had recently put a coffee table in my bedroom. It was painted bright green and it was really smooth. I used to sit there and touch it and feel how smooth it was.'

'They were all blind. Dad took them and shot them all. I heard the shots from my bedroom.'

'So I thought that this coffee table was mine and I really loved it. Then when we moved to another house, the coffee table ended up in the lounge.'

'And the breeding partner dog, he had perfectly fine puppies with another dog, so the problem was with Daisy.'

'And I was fine with it, because the new house was empty, so I thought it was okay for me to let Mum and Dad borrow my table for a while.'

'Dad was so angry. We had to pay thousands of dollars for her to come here and she was worthless to him.'

'Then one day the table disappeared for a while and it came back sanded down. They got rid of the green paint and varnished it.'

'But Mom convinced him to give her another go, so the next year she bred again, and the same thing happened. All white with red eyes again. And he shot them all again.'

'I was so annoyed no one asked me. Because it was my table and they changed it and got rid of the smooth green paint without even asking me. It was still smooth but in a different way. It didn't feel good to touch anymore.'

'And I loved Daisy, more than any of the other dogs, I guess because we got her right when I was the perfect age. I called her Daisy from the beginning, but Dad calls her Gretchen still. He wanted to shoot her too.'

'I didn't make a fuss because it did make more sense in the lounge than in my bedroom. It was right between the couch and the TV and everyone could put their drinks on it. And I could draw or do my homework on it after school in the ad breaks.'

'I cried for days and days and Mom and Dad had a big fight, and Mom convinced him to let Daisy stay. But Dad told me she was my pet, and my responsibility, and he wouldn't walk her or feed her or take her to the vet.'

'But what did annoy me, was as soon as Dad got home from work he would get me to move all my stuff from the table and if I didn't he would pick it up and put it on my bed. And he'd put his feet up on it. It felt really disrespectful.'

'They got her spayed so she couldn't accidentally have any more pups. I had to walk her every day. And I had to feed her. Dad wanted me to pay for her food myself, but I didn't have any money so he said that I'd just have to give her half of all my food. And I did for a while. Mom was furious when she found out Dad told me that.'

'Then one day a few years back I came home from school and the table had gone completely and there was a new one. And no one had asked me about it. And I said, "What happened to my table?" and my dad laughed at me and said, "It wasn't your table."'

'Dad still hates her. When I went to college last year he told me I had to take her with me. But Mom let her stay and looked after her. But since I've been back she's with me again. That's why I got so defensive about her last week.'

'But I was so sure the table was mine. Mum gave it to me. But looking back on it, it was probably not ever mine and that was just something she told me when I was upset. She probably doesn't even remember saying it. So I didn't have anyone to talk to about feeling confused or upset because no one else would understand this feeling. It made me feel useless, like me and my things weren't important. I think that was the day I stopped feeling at home in that house.'

'My story was worse,' she said.

'Yeah, it probably was,' I said.

Then, one day, after we'd spent five weeks in our time zone, she said, 'I have to go back to college next week.'

'Okay,' I said. 'What does that mean for us?'

'I don't know. I need to start sleeping at proper times soon, though.'

'Will you still talk to me?' I asked.

'I'll try.'

'I need to go back to school too. I have probably failed this semester but I'll talk to my teachers and my doctor and see what I can do.'

'Please do,' she said.

'I am going to miss you,' I said. 'You're looking good today, by the way.'

'Am I?' she said. She smiled. She pushed her laptop to the bottom of her bed, kicked up her legs and slowly pulled her shorts off.

'Wow,' I said.

She leaned forward to type, and I saw her bra through the loose neck of her T-shirt. The flashing dots kept appearing and then disappearing on the screen, but when the message appeared it was only one word. 'Sorry.' She shut her laptop. She didn't come back online that day.

The next day she sent me a message. 'I can't do this anymore. I'm going to block you for a while, just until I get things sorted. I promise I'll be back one day.' Then it said she was offline.

I checked the view count on the brushing video every day. It went up by one view every day, but I wasn't sure if that was from me checking on it, or her watching it. I paused the video before it even started playing, so I didn't think it was me. Some days it went up by two, which was a nice feeling. Then it stopped going up at all.

THE WART

I read an article online about how people who read fiction are more empathetic than people who don't, so I switched my major to English literature and got out five classic books from the library. I had gone vegan. I wasn't using any fossil fuels. I was attending all my classes and tutorials. I was exercising regularly. I had a routine.

It was the Tuesday of the fourth week of the new semester. I got up early, ate a light breakfast of toast and peanut butter, did some stretches and ran to university. I didn't have class until the afternoon, so I could sit in my usual spot on the library steps with a pile of books by my side for a few hours. I was aiming to read on average one book every two days. It was doable if I read for four or five hours a day. Whenever I saw a friend on their way into the library I would put my finger on the page I was reading and close my book over it. This was to let them know that I could chat if they wanted, but also that I would be going right back to reading after we stopped talking.

I had developed a rash all over the back of my left wrist from wiping the sweat off my forehead as I ran. I constantly found myself rubbing the rash with my right hand when I was reading. The rash was getting lumpy. I would touch all the lumps and then rub my fingers together to feel the oil from my skin between them. Every time I found a particularly big lump, I squeezed it until pus came out. I didn't carry tissues, so I had to rub the pus back into my skin.

I'd switched to English lit from philosophy. Before that I'd studied sociology, and before that political science. In philosophy I had excelled at formal logic, where I had learned to translate ideas into equations in order to evaluate the validity of them.

One day in a study session, my philosophy friend and I were discussing how we applied formal logic to our day-to-day lives. If everyone studied formal logic, we would all think more rationally and make better decisions.

'What better decisions are you making?' he asked.

'I recycle,' I said.

'Everyone recycles.'

'I don't drive,' I said.

'You don't have a licence, and I drive you around all the time.'

So I stopped accepting rides from him, or from anyone else. The bus cost too much money, so I walked instead. The effort required to walk always seemed like more than the value I got from being somewhere else, so I stopped going out. If I wasn't going to go out there was no point in showering. If I wasn't going to shower there was no point in getting dressed. And if I wasn't going to get dressed there was no point in getting out of bed. The more I thought about it, the more it became apparent that the most rational option was usually to do nothing.

I stopped showing up to my classes and was on the verge of completely flunking out. At that point the only way I could convince myself to leave the house was by promising myself a small bag of lollies from the pick'n'mix.

'But aren't you a vegetarian?' my philosophy friend said when I showed up to a class with my pick'n'mix. To him this was an unbelievable flaw in logic. I was refusing to eat some animal products, but I was still eating lollies that had gelatine in them.

'I know, but I need this,' I said. It didn't matter that I didn't eat meat and that he did; all he cared about was logical consistency. The fact that I cared just made my argument worse, because it meant I was a hypocrite. So I dropped out of philosophy and went vegan.

After reading on the library steps for the morning, I had to decide what to have for lunch. The cheapest vegan meal on campus was three pakora for $3 from the Indian place, but it was only worth going on Mondays and Wednesdays. That was when the generous chef worked, and he made the pakora twice the usual size. A bowl of fries was $5 from the student pub. They were filling, but I had promised Mum when I went vegan that I wouldn't eat chips every day, and I had already eaten chips that week. Sushi wouldn't go half-price until 3pm. The vegan sandwiches at the café were $7 for some lettuce in white bread, the same price as the meat sandwiches and the egg sandwiches. Mum had asked me to please consider eating eggs. I wasn't sure exactly what was wrong with eggs, as long as they were free range, but there were people who knew more about it than me who had chosen not to eat eggs. The supermarket was a ten-minute walk from campus, and I would be able to get a variety of vegan snacks for the same price as a meal. It was the best choice.

I wanted bananas. I knew I should buy fair-trade bananas,

but the fair-trade bananas were twice the price of the unfair bananas and were sold in bunches with stickers that went all the way around, and I only wanted one or two bananas. I had enough money for the fair-trade bananas, but I was on a student budget, so I put two unfair bananas in my basket instead.

The semester before, I would have stopped at the pick'n'mix section next to get a small bag of lollies. The pick'n'mix was always an enjoyable experience. Picking one or two of each lolly, getting the right mix of sour lollies and sweet lollies, finding a good range of different gummy textures – some firm and some soft, some that you could bite right through and some that would get stuck in your teeth. But now I was vegan, so I walked past the pick'n'mix.

In the deli section, the only vegan things were expensive olives. It suddenly occurred to me that the pick'n'mix had more than just lollies. I had to find a new treat, and I did sort of like nuts and seeds. I went back to the pick'n'mix.

Nuts and seeds were not the same pick'n'mix experience as lollies. Each nut had a different code, so I couldn't put them all in the same bag. I could pick but not mix. There were pre-mixed nuts, but they were the same price as cashews even though nearly half of them were peanuts. I ended up picking a small scoop of cashews, a small scoop of Brazil nuts, some almonds, some sunflower seeds, and some peanuts. Each in a separate plastic bag. That seemed like a waste. I'd have to remember to reuse the plastic bags next time I bought nuts. If I was going to use this much plastic, I couldn't get the unfair bananas, so I went back to the fruit and veggie section and swapped them out for the smallest bunch of fair-trade bananas I could find.

I went to the drinks aisle. I could buy a Coke, which was technically vegan but which didn't seem like the right choice. I was not sure about Golden Circle. I put a bottle of lightly flavoured sparkling water in my basket.

I watched at the checkout as the prices of the bags of nuts added up. $3. $4.50. $6. $12. Too many almonds. $13. More than twice what I would pay for a meal on campus, and half my weekly grocery budget. I would have to ration the nuts over three lunches. The bananas were another $4, the sparkling water $1.50. I couldn't fit the bananas in my bag, so I had to carry them around.

I resumed my position on the library steps and ate some nuts and a banana. I looked at the sparkling water and saw that it was manufactured by Coca-Cola. I ripped the label off and buried it at the bottom of my bag. I was meant to have read a book in time for a tutorial that afternoon, but it was 326 pages long and I was already behind on my goal to read a book every two days, so I kept reading *The Bell Jar*, which I was already halfway through.

Since going vegan I had found myself with a lot of energy. I couldn't keep my body still. As I sat on the library steps I bounced my left leg up and down in a constant rhythm, and for each bounce I drummed three fingers down the side of my book, counting to eight and then recounting. I kept catching myself focussing too much on the rhythm and not enough on the words on the page. When I did focus on the words, I had to pause every few sentences to write down my thoughts, which kept interrupting. I wrote them in a notebook, which I kept hidden between the pages of the book so it looked like I was making notes in the margins. I wasn't sure whether writing made me a better person or not. When I looked up from my writing I saw Rosie walking across the courtyard. I wasn't supposed to talk to Rosie, because she'd broken the heart of a friend of mine recently, but she was heading towards me and there was not much I could do. I closed *The Bell Jar* over the notebook and my finger so it would look like I had been reading, but it was clear she had already seen me writing because she said, 'What are you writing?'

'Just notes and thoughts. They might turn into something, maybe a poem or maybe part of a story.'

'I didn't know you were a writer,' Rosie said. 'Can you read me something you've written?'

I read out the thing I had just written in my notebook. 'A man picks at his tooth with his fingernail. He is trying to dig out a piece of nut in there. The man can feel the nut when he closes his mouth. It isn't painful, it doesn't even stop him chewing, but he can feel it. He digs deeper and deeper, lamenting the fact that he cut his fingernails earlier that day. Eventually he realises the nut is not in his top molar where he was picking, but in his bottom one. After this discovery it is easy for him to dig it out.'

'What does it mean?' Rosie asked.

'It doesn't mean just one single thing.'

'Does it mean that sometimes we are looking in the wrong place for solutions to our problems?'

'I don't want to be the type of writer who talks about the meanings in his own work,' I said, but I took note of Rosie's explanation in case I was ever asked to explain it again.

'Hmm,' Rosie said. 'Interesting.'

'Do you want a banana?' I asked. 'I bought too many.' I held the bunch out to her. There were still five left. 'You can take two.'

She took one, and continued into the library. I tried to extract the piece of nut from my bottom molar. When I'd realised it was in there rather than in the top one, I had rushed to write down what was happening without actually trying to get it out. It turned out it was still much harder to remove than I had imagined.

I finished *The Bell Jar* ten minutes before my tutorial was due to start. As we were waiting outside the classroom to be let in, I read half the essay about ironic realism that we were going to be discussing alongside the book I had not read.

The tutor asked the class if we could come up with an example of ironic reality from the book I had not read.

A girl sitting near me brought up the most photographed barn in America. She said, 'The barn both does and does not exist. You can only see the barn if you have never heard of the barn, but because it's so well known no one can see it.'

'It's kind of like *The Bell Jar*,' I said.

'What do you mean by that?' my tutor asked.

'Well, I think *The Bell Jar* is underrated as a comedy,' I said.

'Why do you think *The Bell Jar* is a comedy?'

'Because it's funny,' I said.

'I don't think it's funny at all,' said the girl from before.

'That's what I mean by it being underrated as a comedy,' I said. 'Everyone has heard that it's so sad, so no one reads it as a comedy, which means no one thinks it's funny. Our perception of *The Bell Jar* is based on how everyone talks about it. Just like the barn. That makes it ironic.'

'I think we are getting off track,' the tutor said.

The class went back to talking about the ironic barn. I sat back in my chair and touched my arm. I had already squeezed most of the big bumps and they had scabbed over. I picked at the scabs. Some of them fell away easily and others started bleeding. I rubbed the blood into my skin. I felt a small lump on the back of my hand, smaller than the bumps. I squeezed it, but nothing happened. It felt deeper than the bumps. It felt more serious.

I was still squeezing the lump when everyone else got up to leave. I grabbed all my things from the desk and left the room as quickly as I could so my tutor couldn't ask me to explain myself. Tonight I would read the book I hadn't read, even if I had to stay up all night.

As I was leaving the campus, I ducked into the student medical centre and requested an appointment with my doctor. The receptionist asked if it was urgent and I paused for a long time. I still had a repeat left on my prescription, so I wouldn't need new antidepressants for another month. Eventually she said she would mark it as urgent, and gave me an appointment for the next morning.

That night I managed to read three-quarters of the book I hadn't read. Or, I looked at three-quarters of the words in the book in order, while rubbing a finger over the lump on the back of my hand. I did not get to sleep until 4am.

The next morning I got up early, had a light breakfast of peanut butter on toast, packed my bag with my pencil case, notebook, drink bottle, a change of clothes and my leftover nuts, did some stretches, put on my running playlist and set off on my run to uni. I carried my backpack over one shoulder to stop my back sweat from soaking into it, switching shoulders every five minutes as they got sore.

Halfway to uni there was a river. As I approached the bridge I had to put my iPod in my pocket, because I always got the urge to throw it over the railing. I had never actually done it, but today the urge was stronger than it had ever been before. I pushed my iPod deeper into my pocket with my thumb, which made my headphones tug on my ears, so I had to crouch my body down as I ran. This only increased the urge to throw my iPod into the river. I took my thumb out of my pocket and sprinted until I was well clear of the bridge.

A bus drove past and I did a quick jump away from the road to counter my urge to jump in front of it. I knew I was never going to jump in front of a bus, but I still had to protect myself. The urges were no longer frightening, but they were becoming more frequent. I always ran along the main roads, where all the trucks and buses went. I could have followed the river around the loop and through the park instead and then cut through a small patch of native bush to arrive at the uni gates. It would have made a much nicer journey, but it would take an extra ten minutes. It made more sense to take the most direct route.

When I arrived at uni I made my way to the disabled toilet on the fourth floor of the science block. It was close to the entrance of the university, and I had never seen it occupied. Before I went in I checked the floor to make sure there were no people in wheelchairs or with crutches as they might need the toilet more than me. I didn't want to take their space, but the disabled toilets were the only ones with paper towels in the cubicles.

I stripped naked and wet several paper towels in the sink. I wiped my body down with the wet paper towels, then put a little bit of pump soap under my armpits and crotch and anywhere else that seemed particularly sweaty. I wiped the soap off my body with more wet paper towels, then dried off with fresh paper towels. I repeated the process two or three times until I had stopped sweating. Then I sprayed on deodorant, changed into my clean clothes and put my dirty ones in a plastic bag, which I reused every day, and shoved it deep into the bottom of my bag before heading to the medical centre.

'Is everything okay?' my doctor asked.

'I've gone vegan,' I said.

'Do you think you're getting a balanced diet?' she asked.

'I think so,' I said. 'I've done a lot of reading about it.'

'It's not really my area of expertise,' she said. 'I could find some pamphlets if you want.'

'No, it's okay. I'm eating lots of beans. I'm trying really hard to be better,' I said.

'That's good to hear,' she said. 'You seem to be in good spirits.'

We sat for a moment in silence.

'Was there anything else?' she asked.

'I'm worried about this lump on my hand,' I said. I showed her my arm. Most of the rash had scabbed over. I hadn't realised how severe it looked till now.

'No, not that stuff. That's just a rash,' I said. 'This one.' I pointed at the white lump on the back of my hand.

She looked at it for a long time. 'This looks like a wart,' she said eventually. 'Have you had warts before?'

'No. Never,' I said. 'What should I do about it?'

'We could burn it off,' she said, 'but I'm reluctant to do that yet. Not until it becomes an issue.'

'Okay.'

'Is it bothering you?'

'I guess it's not an issue,' I said.

'It's good you came in, just to check,' she said. She printed out another prescription for my antidepressants even though I didn't need one yet, and then she stood up, so I stood up too and then I left.

I went back to my spot on the library steps to finish the book for class. The girl from my tutorial walked up the steps and smiled at me. I put my finger in the book and closed it over the top of it and smiled back at her. She walked into the library and I went back to reading. When I finished the book I added it to the reading log I was keeping at the back of my notebook. I went into the library and read a summary of the book on the internet. I ate a bowl of chips for lunch.

I arrived at my lecture early. I always arrived at lectures early. I sat at the seat closest to the door, which meant every student who wanted to sit in the back row had to squeeze past me. I should have moved to the centre, but I wanted to be able to leave if I needed to. I had to sit at the back because I didn't like people looking at me. I brought the newly read book to the lecture, but the lecturer moved on to another book I hadn't read yet. I looked at my hand. I tried to cover the wart with my other hand, but then I could feel it.

I scraped the wart with a broken piece of ruler that I had in my pencil case. The skin around the wart went white, but the wart didn't change. After a few seconds the skin turned pink again and the wart looked white in comparison. I did this a few times, trying to work out if the wart was changing colour itself or if it was just the skin around it.

The wart wasn't doing any harm, but it also wasn't doing any good. I knew it was not one of the main things I should be worried about, but it was still there, sitting on my hand, making everything a little bit worse.

I poked at the wart with a pencil.

I looked up and the lecturer was talking about the argument that we were not only living in an era of postmodernism, but in an era of postmodernity. That after the bombings of Hiroshima and Nagasaki, nothing could be the same. Personally, though, he tended to disagree.

The problem with the wart wasn't that it was painful, or itchy, or even that it looked bad, but that I could always feel it was there. I sharpened the pencil, putting the shavings into my pencil case, then I poked at the wart again. It didn't react. I pushed the pencil hard into the wart. Any other part of my skin would have been pierced by the pencil, but the skin of the wart was thick. The pencil lead broke.

I took a compass out of my pencil case. The compass had been in there since high school, and all it had done since then was poke me whenever I picked up my pencil case. The tip of the compass broke the skin of the wart with only a little bit of pressure. I used the compass to push the wart around and around in small circles. The wart grew redder. I took the compass out of the wart and a speck of blood seeped out. I rubbed the blood into my skin. I put the compass back into the hole and pushed it further in until the whole tip of the compass was inside my hand. I tried to scoop the wart out. My skin tore and I made a sound. I covered the wart with my other hand and looked at the person next to me. He was looking at the lecturer.

The lecturer was reading a passage from the new book I had not read, emphasising the word 'before', which came at the beginning of each sentence. I looked at my book and tried finding the section he was reading from, but the page numbers were different because I bought my copy online. The blood was starting to pool on my hand.

I licked my hand clean and sucked the blood away from the wart. I looked at it and there was a white lump sitting amongst the blood. I pushed the compass into the skin next to the white lump. New blood came out of the new puncture. I dragged the compass around the lump, ripping up all the skin. I made another sound. I looked up.

The lecturer had stopped talking and was looking at me. The person next to me was looking at me. Most of the people in the class had turned around and were looking at me. I grabbed my book and pencil case and bag and ran out of the lecture theatre.

I held my pencil case to the hole in my hand as I ran back to the disabled bathroom on the fourth floor of the science block. I dropped everything onto the floor and rinsed my hand in the sink. My pencil case was covered in blood and that blood was smeared all over the floor. I tried to wipe it up but as I cleaned I dripped more blood. I looked at the wart. It was still a white lump in the middle of a bloody wound. I tried squeezing it, but I had cut my fingernails the day before and I couldn't get a grip on it. I put my mouth around the wound and sucked all the blood away. I looked at the wart again, and then I positioned my teeth around it and bit down hard. I pulled my hand away from my mouth and the wart came out at the root, leaving a deep hole in the back of my hand. I sat on the toilet and watched the hole fill with blood.

I tried to clean up the blood on the floor as best I could, but all I did was smear it around. I took a few pens out of my pencil case before throwing it into the bin. I had made the pencil case when I was twelve years old in sewing class and had kept it all through high school. It was covered in the names of all the bands I'd loved as a fourteen-year-old in Vivid, and the names of all the bands I'd loved as a sixteen-year-old in Twink. I left the science block as quietly as I could, apologising in my head to the cleaners who would have to deal with the mess I had made. I wandered around the quieter parts of campus holding a paper towel to the back of my hand, hoping I wouldn't see anyone from my lecture. Eventually I decided it would be a good idea to go back to the medical centre.

The receptionist quickly ushered me into a side room and a nurse came and cleaned up my wound and put a bandage on it.

'What have you done here?' she said over and over.

'It isn't a big deal,' I tried saying, but I couldn't because I was crying.

'Wait here. I need to go and get someone,' she said. 'I need to go and get your doctor.'

So I waited. I took the new book out of my bag and started reading. My next class was in a couple of days and I was going to catch up in time.

FLATMATES

It was 7:30 in the morning when Clara woke me up by bashing on a cowbell outside my room, yelling 'Flat meeting' repeatedly.

I rolled out of bed and found a T-shirt on the floor and pulled it over my body. I found a pair of shorts under my bed and put them on as I left my bedroom.

'What the hell is this about, Clara,' Faith said. She was standing in her bedroom door in her pyjamas.

'Just get out here,' Clara said. 'Duncan too.'

I came out of my room and sat on the couch. Clara was standing up. She was wearing a grey skirt, a white shirt, black stockings and black leather shoes with a slight heel. I hadn't seen her in these clothes before because she always came home via the gym, and I hadn't gotten up this early in a long time. 'Wait here,' she said. 'Don't you dare go back to bed.'

Faith led Duncan into the lounge. He hadn't put any clothes over the tattered underwear he slept in. He had bed hair, but he always had bed hair. He had a depression beard. He had so much body hair it was a wonder he ever needed clothes. He sat on the couch and pulled Ugly Blanket: The Ugliest Blanket in the World over him. We had named it Ugly Blanket: The Ugliest Blanket in the World because it was exactly that. It was an old polar-fleece blanket with a bright pink and aqua pattern of round splotches and cartoonish flower shapes that barely fitted together. It was too thin to be warm and too small to cover an entire body, but it had become a permanent fixture on the couch. We had discussed getting rid of it but since no one else in the world would ever want it, it felt cruel.

'What's happening?' Duncan asked.

Clara appeared in the lounge again holding our toothbrush mug. 'Why the hell do we have twelve toothbrushes? There are only four of us living here.'

'Three,' I said.

'Is this really why you got us up, Clara,' Faith said.

Clara put the mug down on the coffee table. 'I'm tired of this. I can't live in filth anymore.'

'There are only three of us living here,' I said.

'Plus Duncan,' Clara said.

'Duncan doesn't live here,' Faith said.

'Duncan pretty much lives here,' Clara said.

'No. We talked about it and decided we weren't ready to move in together,' Duncan said. He yawned.

'Faith,' I said, 'does Duncan live with us?'

'Yes. How have you missed this,' Clara said. 'He's been here every day for months.'

'No he doesn't,' Faith said. 'Duncan lives with his dad.'

'Duncan's dad. The one in Palmerston North?' Clara said.

'If Duncan is going to be living here we should renegotiate rent,' I said.

'I don't have time for this,' Clara said. 'Everyone grab your toothbrush. I need to get to work.'

'I thought you woke us up for a flat meeting,' I said.

'No, I woke you up to clean up these stupid toothbrushes.' Clara looked at the mug. 'Grab your toothbrush. We're throwing the rest out.' She took a green toothbrush from the mug. It looked barely used.

Faith found her pink brush. 'How did we get so many brushes?' she said.

Duncan looked at the mug for a while and then pulled out a worn blue toothbrush with dried toothpaste around the handle.

'What the hell,' I said. 'That's my toothbrush.' I looked into the mug and saw a very similar toothbrush that was a slightly lighter shade of blue. 'That must be your one there.'

'I'm pretty sure this is my one,' he said. 'I'm like 65 percent sure.'

'That's not sure enough to use a toothbrush,' I said.

'Well, I was more sure than that up until a minute ago,' Duncan said.

Faith and Clara laughed.

'You don't even live here,' I said.

'Exactly. He doesn't live here,' Faith said.

'You all need to stop pretending Duncan doesn't live here,' Clara said.

Duncan yawned.

'He should be paying rent,' I said.

'He can't afford to pay rent,' Faith said. 'He doesn't have a job.'

'I don't have a job,' I said.

'Yeah, but you're doing okay,' Faith said. 'You're not missing rent.'

'What about our bills,' I said. 'He uses our shower and the internet.'

'I don't really shower that much,' Duncan said.

'And you use the internet more than any of us,' Faith said.

'Okay.' I pulled out my phone and opened the calculator. 'If Clara and I pay $25 less a week each, then you and Duncan can pay $50 more.'

'I don't have time to deal with this,' Clara said. 'I need to get to work.'

'We'd have to take Duncan's situation into account,' Faith said, 'to make it fair.'

'$50 is taking that into account,' I said. 'It's fair.'

'I don't even care,' Clara said. 'I just want you all to clean up after yourselves whether you're living here or not.' She took her toothbrush back to the bathroom and left out the back door, leaving the mug of remaining toothbrushes on the table for us to deal with.

Clara was the only one in the flat who could afford a car. She was the only one who had regular work hours and the only one who always did her chores on time.

She had studied marketing at university, even though she hated it. She said she didn't want to get into tens of thousands of dollars of debt for something that wasn't going to pay the bills. I told her that I wished I was that sensible and she said that she felt like she didn't have a choice but to be sensible. She grew up with a solo mum and didn't have anyone to fall back on. She got a job straight out of uni at an advertising company. She did admin work but it had potential for growth into the future.

'Should we throw these out then?' I said.

'I guess so,' Faith said.

I picked up the remaining toothbrushes. They were wet and had black sludge dripping from the bottoms.

'What about our one, Duncan?' I said.

'You don't want to keep it?' he said.

'No. Gross.'

'I'll hang on to it until I get a new one then.'

'Duncan, please throw out the toothbrush,' Faith said. 'I'll buy you a new one today.'

I picked up the mug and showed the others the layer of black sludge that had formed in its bottom. 'What should we do with this?' I said.

'We need a new mug,' Faith said.

'I'll clean it,' Duncan said as he curled up on the couch. Ugly Blanket only just fitted over his torso, and his bare legs stuck out.

'Duncan, go back to bed,' Faith said.

'I'm awake now,' he said. 'I'll make us breakfast.'

I took the toothbrushes to the bathroom and threw them in the bin next to the toilet. I looked in the mirror. My teeth were yellow. I had forgotten to brush them the night before and now I couldn't use my brush. It had been a week since I last shaved. I took the hand soap, the floss and Clara's toothbrush from next to the sink and put it on the windowsill by the toilet so I didn't make a mess. I didn't have shaving cream so I lathered up my face with soap and shaved. I drained the sink and wiped it down with some toilet paper to get rid of most of the hairs from shaving. It was still early so I decided to go back to bed.

As I went back through the lounge Faith was sitting on top of Duncan's legs and eating a bowl of muesli. Duncan had a bowl of muesli sitting on his chest and was struggling to get the spoon into his mouth in that position. I went back to bed and heard Faith pack up her things and leave.

———

Faith worked at a café in town. She had worked in cafés all through uni and then found a more or less full-time job in one afterwards. She talked about going back to do postgrad but wasn't sure if she could afford it.

The first time Faith met her boss he had waited patiently in line, then politely asked for a latte and a pastry. Faith had carefully watched the espresso pour, steamed the milk perfectly, and then made a perfect fern on top. She'd rung up the order and told him the amount, and instead of handing over money, he'd given her his business card, featuring the logo of the café, his name, and the word 'Owner'.

'Does this mean you don't have to pay?' Faith asked.

'That is correct.'

'Okay, well, I hope you enjoy your coffee.'

'I'm going to need that card back, I'm running out.'

The café was started by his ex-girlfriend, who hired Faith but got bankrolled by him, and when they broke up he fired her and decided to take a more hands-on approach to the business, which meant moving in to the office out the back. All the supervisors ended up doing the work that the manager used to do, but for less pay. Faith had no idea what her boss did in the back office for most the day but everything went better when he stayed out there.

Faith had taken to stealing things from the café. She always ordered too much milk and would bring home litres that were close to expiry. The leftover pastries were meant to be ripped up and thrown in with the coffee grinds, but she always managed to save a few of them for us. She brought home teaspoons that weren't needed and once brought home a whole set of drinking glasses that had been sitting in the storeroom since before she started.

———

I lay in bed with my eyes closed for half an hour but I was paranoid about falling asleep and missing my alarm. I had a WINZ appointment I needed to be at in a couple of hours. I got out of bed and went to the kitchen. I looked at my shelf in the pantry. All I had was a bag of rice and a can of tomato sauce. I considered stealing some of Faith's muesli, but there was no milk left to eat it with. I went to the bathroom and looked in the mirror. My neck was covered in red bumps from shaving and my teeth looked even worse. I tried to scrape the plaque off my teeth with my fingernails. It didn't work so I put some toothpaste on my finger and smeared it on my teeth. My teeth squeaked as I polished each one with a circular motion. I took a sip of water from the tap and swished it around my mouth and spat it out. I grinned in the mirror. My teeth were still yellow.

Duncan had fallen asleep on the couch. He had pulled his legs right up to his chest to fit them under Ugly Blanket and had tucked it underneath him so it stretched over him tightly like a cocoon.

I smelled the T-shirts on my bedroom floor one by one until I found one that was clean and then I left the house.

I liked Duncan. He was more like a piece of furniture than a flatmate. I wasn't resentful that he was living with us, but I didn't know how to tell him that I'd prefer him to wear clothes around the house. He had dropped out of uni because he got depressed. Every new semester since then, he re-enrolled and showed up to the first week of classes before withdrawing again. I didn't know how he and Faith met, but Faith seemed to like looking after him. He used to spend all his days in Faith's room as quietly as possible, but eventually he started coming out to the lounge to hang out with me during the day. We had an old PlayStation with only one controller, so Duncan and

I took turns watching the other play. The only games we had were nearly twenty years old. I had to be talked through the games by Duncan, who had mastered them all as a kid. I once told him that I had dropped out of uni a couple of times too, but he didn't seem to want to talk about it.

I stopped by Faith's café for a free coffee on my way to WINZ. At first it was a bit of a gamble to show up there because if Faith's boss was around she would charge me unexpectedly, but eventually she worked out if she pretended to punch things into the till and then opened and closed the cash register, he would have no idea I hadn't paid.

Faith brought my coffee over to me and sat down. Her workmate Nicola had finished washing dishes out the back and took over the till.

'What have you got on today?' Faith asked.

'WINZ appointment,' I said.

'I should get Duncan to sign up for the dole,' Faith said. 'But he thinks he's going to go back to uni soon so there's no point.'

'Yeah, I guess it would be a good idea,' I said.

'If he did, we could afford more rent,' Faith said.

I tossed up whether to agree with her or tell her it wasn't a big deal, but before I said anything Faith's boss drifted out of his back office. His pants were too big. They went all the way to the ground, covering his shoes. Faith said it was because his feet were tiny and he was trying to hide them. He didn't lift his feet up while walking, and his steps were smooth and continuous, so it looked like he was gliding. He walked with his hands in his pockets.

'Faith, can you make me a latte please?' he said.

Nicola was at the coffee machine already, but he always

got Faith to make his coffee. He said she was the best. Nicola grabbed a cloth and started wiping the bench.

I watched Faith make the coffee. Her boss stood right behind her. 'I want to see how you do it,' he said.

I walked the long way around town to WINZ to kill time, but I still arrived half an hour early. I bought a vegetarian sausage roll, a toothbrush and a single serving of squeeze-on tomato sauce from the dairy across the road. The toothbrush didn't have a price on it and when I took it to the counter it was $6.50. It felt too late to take it back. I put the toothbrush in my pocket and went for a walk around the block to give me time to eat the veggie sausage roll. I got back to WINZ with twenty minutes to spare. I considered dry brushing my teeth in the street but that would make me look crazy, so I went for a second walk around the block.

I was twelve minutes early when I walked into WINZ, but there was a line that reached the door. In front of me there was a young mother holding a toddler. The toddler looked at me and licked her lips. When the young mother got to the front of the queue the toddler started crying and the mother was trying to calm her while talking to the receptionist. Eventually she took the toddler aside and gave up her place in line and I went up to the counter.

'Can I help you?' the receptionist asked.

'Yes, I got a letter which told me to come in today.' The letter had said to bring it to the office with me but I had lost it. I gave the receptionist my community services card number.

'You're ten minutes late,' she said.

'I was here on time but the line was long,' I said.

'If you showed up at a job interview ten minutes late what would they say?'

55

'I'm not usually late,' I said.

'Take a seat. A case manager will be with you shortly.'

I sat in the waiting area. The plastic packaging of the toothbrush dug into my thigh so I took it out of my pocket and held on to it.

When I finished uni I went to the doctor and they gave me a medical certificate saying I wasn't well enough to work full-time. She told me that it was just to buy me time to find a job that I could manage. I did not find a job I could manage. Even the most basic job required experience and seemed overwhelming. When my medical certificate expired I had to meet with a case manager to prove I was looking for work.

I told her I hoped not to need WINZ support for long. I just needed a bit of time to find the right job.

'First off we are not called WINZ,' the case manager said. 'If you have a look at our website you will not see a single mention of WINZ. And, secondly, you're not here to find the right job. Finding the right job can come later.'

'Sorry,' I said.

'Do you have any skills that would help you find work?' she asked.

'I've just finished a degree,' I said.

'And what skills do you have that would help you find employment?'

'I can write,' I said. 'I majored in English literature and I minored in creative writing.'

'Would you be interested in doing a course in hospitality or retail?'

'I have skills,' I said. 'I just need to find a job for them.'

———

It was twenty minutes before my name was called out. I introduced myself to the case manager.

'I'm your case manager for today,' he said. His name tag said 'Case Manager'. I followed him to his workstation in the middle of the room. The desk had brown plastic strips around the side and a veneer top.

'Please take a seat,' the case manager said.

I introduced myself again, hoping to find out his name.

'We have stopped using our names here because of security concerns,' he said.

'Okay.' I put the toothbrush on the desk.

He typed on his computer. 'I'm just pulling up your file. It won't be a minute.'

I felt my chair starting to sink towards the ground. I could see the inside of the case manager's nostrils.

'So, we called you in here today because you've been on Jobseeker Support for coming up fifty-two weeks now.'

I was surprised by this, but realised it had been. 'Uh huh,' I said.

'There's a policy here that at fifty-two weeks our jobseekers have to reapply for the benefit.'

'Yes. Okay. I can do that.'

'Okay, so are all your details the same? Phone number? Address?'

'Yes, they should be the same,' I said. My chair was sinking. The case manager hit enter half a dozen times in a row.

'Oh, okay, we seem to have hit a problem here. We can't seem to reapply for the jobseeker benefit, as you're currently receiving a benefit.'

'Well, yes,' I said. 'That's why I'm here.'

'Hmmm. Okay. I'm just going to cancel your current benefit right here. Then we should be able to move forward with your reapplication.'

'If that's what you have to do,' I said. I stood and pulled the lever on the chair to make it rise.

The case manager typed on his keyboard. He did not look concerned. I picked up my toothbrush and read about how I should angle the toothbrush and my head in order to best reach my back teeth. I practised opening my jaw and touched the back of my teeth with my tongue.

'Okay, you have reapplied,' he said. 'Everything should be sorted now.'

'Okay, will the benefit come through on Monday as usual?'

'I'll just check that.' He typed on the keyboard again. 'Oops, there seems to be something wrong here. You are required to attend a seminar on jobseeking before your next payment. I'll just book you into one.' He hit enter on the keyboard several times in a row, then scribbled a time and date on a business card. 'Your benefit will be reinstated after this date.' The date was three weeks later. My chair sank.

'But I have to pay rent,' I said. 'I can't live without any money for three weeks.'

'Yes, that is an issue. It shouldn't have done that. I'll see if I can fix it.'

'Thank you,' I said.

The desk had one of those holes covered with two moon-shaped plastic bits that you could swivel around and put computer cables through, but the case manager's cables were just hanging off the edge of the desk. I swivelled the bits so that the hole opened. I dropped my toothbrush through the hole and tried to catch it from underneath but I missed and it fell on the ground.

'Nope, it doesn't look like there is anything I can do from this position, but what we can do is go over some budgeting advice.' My chair sank. The case manager searched through a drawer and put a pamphlet in front of me. 'Have a read of this,' he said. The pamphlet was called 'Living Within Our Means: A Guide to Basic Household Budgeting'.

'I have rent to pay,' I said.

'So what I'm hearing is rent is an issue.'

'Yes, it is an issue.'

'I'm just going to see if you're eligible for an accommodation supplement.' He typed on his computer. I tried to find my toothbrush by patting my foot around on the floor without looking away from the case manager's face. I thought I had it but it was one of the cables. 'Unfortunately,' he said, 'you're no longer eligible for an accommodation supplement.'

'What happened?'

'We can work it out later, but for now let's go over your budget. How much is your rent?'

'It's $170 a week.'

He opened the pamphlet on the desk and pointed to a table on the second page. 'It says here that you should be aiming to spend less than 50 percent of your income on rent,' he said.

'But that's not possible. There are no rooms available for that little.'

'That may be, but $170 a week is the level we'd expect for someone earning more than $340 a week. It's all about living within our means. When I was a child I shared a bedroom with my brother and that never did me any harm. You don't know someone who can share your bedroom? A friend or maybe a partner?'

'I don't have a partner.' My chair sank.

'We all have to learn how to live within our means.'

'Yes but the problem isn't my living, it's my means. I have no means. I can't live within no means.'

I stood up and pulled the lever again so the chair rose. 'Just leave it,' the case manager said. 'The chair is broken and it's not going to be fixed by doing the same thing again and again.' I pulled the lever without standing up and the chair sank even lower so that my chin only just reached up to the desk.

I had a text from Clara asking if I was in town and if I could help her with something.

I met her in a park near her work. She was holding a stack of big folders and was sweaty. 'I was told to deliver these files around town,' she said. 'They said it would only take half an hour, but I'm not even halfway and it's been forty-five minutes.'

Clara took off her shoes. She had red welts around the back of her heels. 'I was going to put on my gym shoes, but my boss was watching me, so I didn't.'

'Can I help?' I said. 'I can help.'

'I don't even know why they're getting me to do this,' she said. 'We usually get couriers to deliver everything.'

'That sucks,' I said.

She opened a can of tuna. 'Do you mind if I eat this here? I didn't get a lunch break.'

'No, go ahead.' It smelled very strong. 'I can deliver some of them,' I said.

'No, that would be weird,' she said. 'I should do them myself.'

'Do you want me to hold them for you?' I asked.

'No,' she said. 'Just give me a moment and I'll do them.'

'Why did you need me?' I asked.

'I'm not sure anymore,' she said. 'But thanks.'

I wanted to tell her that I didn't have any way of paying rent this week, but she did a big sigh and put her head in her hands.

I sat there with her for a minute or so before she jumped up and said, 'Better get back to it,' and left.

When I got home I was surprised to find that the lounge was clean. The morning's muesli bowls were gone, as were the half dozen mugs that had been covering every surface. The floor had been vacuumed, the stray letters had been stacked into piles according to which flatmate they belonged to, and the cushions had been fluffed and elegantly placed on the couch. The only thing out of place was the toothbrush mug still sitting on the coffee table.

I was not surprised to see Duncan had not gotten dressed. He was sitting upright on the couch in his pair of ratty underwear and had Ugly Blanket hanging around his neck like a cape.

'Did you do this?' I asked.

'Yes,' he said. 'I should be helping out a bit more, if I'm going to stay here so often.'

'Thank you,' I said. 'You know no one minds that you're staying here, right?' Duncan looked down to avoid eye contact.

'What's the best way to clean gunk out of a mug?' Duncan asked.

'I would probably just leave it to soak,' I said.

'I want it to be clean before Faith gets home,' he said. He jumped up and grabbed the mug. Ugly Blanket swooped around as he turned to go to the kitchen.

The kitchen had also been cleaned. All of the dishes had been done and put away. The tiles behind the stove no longer had oil and tomato marks all over them. I watched Duncan scrape the gunk out of the edge of the mug with a knife, then he pushed a scouring pad right to the bottom of the mug and twisted it around his hand.

The bathroom had also been cleaned. The toilet was not yellow around the bottom and there were no black curly hairs at the bottom of the shower. The only thing on the sinktop was Faith's pink toothbrush. Everything else was still on the windowsill. I tapped my pockets and realised I had left my new toothbrush on the floor at WINZ.

Duncan appeared in the doorway. 'Do you think Faith would mind if I used her toothbrush?' he said.

'Uhhh,' I said. 'Probably.'

'Because I have already used it,' he said.

I looked at Duncan. 'I think you've got something in your beard,' I said.

Duncan reached up and ran his hands through his beard and found a small pill. 'Oops, it's my antidepressant. Looks like I'm gonna be sad tomorrow.'

Faith brought home six litres of milk that afternoon. She carried one two-litre bottle in each hand and one in her backpack. She dumped them on the coffee table.

'Did you bring any food home?' I asked.

She reached into her bag and pulled out six brown paper bags. She threw me one with a pizza scroll in it. She also pulled out a mug with her café's name printed on it and put it on the table. 'For the toothbrushes,' she said.

'I cleaned the toothbrush mug,' Duncan said. 'It took ages but I did it.' He pulled the mug out from underneath Ugly Blanket and placed it on the coffee table with a flourish. Now there were two mugs on the table. 'But we can use your new one if you want.'

Faith looked at the old mug. There was a hair on it. 'No, you went to all that effort. We'll keep using it.'

I took the bags of food, Faith's new mug and the milk to

the kitchen. I opened the cupboard to put the mug on the mug shelf. There was no room for it. We did not need a new mug. I checked the expiry dates on the milk. One of the bottles was expiring the next day and the other two weren't expiring for another week. I didn't want to waste any milk so I poured some of the almost-expired milk into the new mug and took it back to the lounge.

Duncan and I played PlayStation. He talked me through how to get past the level I was on, but I kept dying early. When I got down to my last life I gave the controller to Duncan to complete the level.

Faith appeared in the doorway holding her toothbrush. 'Duncan,' she said, 'did you use my toothbrush today? It's wet.'

'Oh. Uh. Yes,' he said. 'I thought you wouldn't mind because . . . you know . . . we kiss and stuff.' Duncan got past the part of the level I kept dying at. He smiled. His teeth were quite disgusting.

'Well, I'd rather you didn't,' she said. She threw her toothbrush at him, but it went down the back of the couch.

'Did you get a new one today?' Duncan asked.

'Sorry, I forgot,' Faith said. She sat down next to Duncan. 'Nicola quit today.'

'Why did she quit?' I asked.

'My boss is a dick,' Faith said.

'Aren't all bosses dicks?' Duncan said. He was up to the Boss at the end of the level.

'He's a massive dick.' Faith lay down on the couch. Duncan lifted up the controller so there was room on his lap for her head. 'Nicola decided she didn't want to put up with it anymore.' She pulled Ugly Blanket from him and hugged it. 'But I got a promotion,' she said. 'I'm now officially the café manager.'

'That's awesome,' I said.

'I guess so,' she said. 'I couldn't really say no.'

'You shouldn't be modest,' Duncan said. 'You deserve it.' The Boss had 10 percent health left. Duncan was going to win.

'I can probably pay a bit more rent now. For Duncan too.'

'We should do something to celebrate,' Duncan said. He'd beaten the Boss and completed the level with 100 percent of the goals.

'I'm tired,' Faith said. Duncan saved the game and put the controller down.

'Now I'm meant to find someone else to work there too,' Faith said.

'I'm looking for a job,' I said.

'He usually hires women,' Faith said. 'But maybe.' Faith turned around and pushed her head into Duncan's chest.

'Did you notice I cleaned up,' Duncan asked as he rubbed the back of Faith's head.

'I did,' Faith said. 'You've done a great job.'

In my room I took my laptop out and looked up jobs websites. I looked through the drop-down list, but couldn't make up my mind, so I selected 'All Categories'. I also selected 'Any Job Type' rather than 'Full Time', because even though I was meant to be looking for full-time work, I'd take what I could get. In the salary section I selected '$0 to $50K', then I changed my mind and selected '$0 to $35K'. I also looked under 'Flatmates Wanted' for rooms under $120 a week.

I opened a new tab for every job mentioning 'Sales Superstars', 'Customer Service Officers', 'Receptionists', 'Creatives', 'Corrections Officers', 'Front of House Staff', 'Cleaners' and 'Personal Assistants'. I didn't click on anything with the words 'Manager', 'Supervisor' or 'Senior' in it.

I read the job ads but every single one required experience or proven skills that I couldn't prove. I closed the browser. I opened the door to the lounge and noticed that Duncan had hung the cowbell on a 3M hook on the wall above the couch. Underneath it, Faith was on top of Duncan. 'Do it quick,' she said quietly. Duncan was just as naked as usual and Faith was more naked than usual. Ugly Blanket was barely covering them. I closed the door before they saw me. I needed to pee. I put my ear to the door and could hear light panting and moving, and the gentle dinging of the cowbell. I climbed out of my bedroom window into the backyard, and peed against a tree near the fence.

'Disgusting,' I heard Clara say. She was sitting at the old picnic table that the last tenants had left in the yard.

I turned away from her. 'Sorry, I just had to go,' I said. I finished peeing and zipped up my fly. 'I was trapped. Faith and Duncan were –'

'Yeah, I know,' she said. 'I tried to get in just before.'

'Why the lounge?' I said.

'Sometimes you've just gotta do it I guess.'

'And I'm the disgusting one,' I said.

'You're all disgusting,' she said.

I sat down opposite her. She was eating tuna out of a can with her fingers. Several more cans of tuna were stacked in front of her.

'How did the deliveries go?' I said.

'It took forever,' she said. 'Every time I got to a new office I was asked if I took the stairs, or if I ran there, and I didn't. I'm just sweaty.'

'You're not that sweaty,' I said.

'By the time I got back to the office everyone had left and there was a letter on my desk reminding me that today was the last day of my internship. It has been a year.'

'I didn't know you were an intern,' I said.

'I thought it might turn into a proper job,' she said, 'so I never told anyone it was just an internship. No one had mentioned the end of my contract coming up so I thought it had slipped their mind. I thought if I kept showing up and kept working, no one would notice. But they did.' She opened another can of tuna.

'I guess so,' I said.

'I don't know what I'm going to do. I'm paying off my phone and laptop and I haven't even started paying off the car yet.' She picked up a lump of tuna from the can and put it in her mouth. 'I'll have to pay rent with my credit card next week.'

'How did you get a credit card?'

'They'll give anyone a credit card,' she said. 'You just have to ask.'

'They had already locked me out of my emails and my files when I got back. I spent an hour pretending to tidy up my things but I didn't have much to pack up. Only these cans of tuna. They were meant to last me till the end of the week.' She scooped a handful of tuna from the can and ate it out of the palm of her hand. 'I opened one in the office and smeared a bit of tuna on the undersides of the cupboards in the kitchen and in the crisper drawer of the fridge and under the plate of the microwave. Then I poured the brine onto my boss's carpet.' Clara tipped the can up and drank the brine and last few pieces of tuna from the can. She went to open another one.

'Can you please eat something else?' I asked.

'This is all I have,' she said.

'Faith brought home some food,' I said. 'It's in the kitchen. If we can get in there.'

'The back door's locked,' she said. 'I've checked.'

66

We looked for another way in. The bathroom window was ajar. I unlatched it and tried to pull myself up into it. I couldn't do it, so Clara pushed me from behind. As I climbed in, I kicked over the hand soap that was sitting on the windowsill. It fell onto the floor and soap spilled everywhere. I reached out the window and gave Clara my hand. She grabbed it and I leaned back, pulling her up. She got a foot onto the windowsill and climbed up, kicking over the floss and her toothbrush, which fell into the toilet.

'Sorry,' I said.

Clara laughed. Her breath smelled like tuna.

DEBTS

I have not paid rent for six weeks. My flatmates are not happy. They pound on my door saying they know I'm in there, but I don't answer. I keep my door locked at all times and climb in and out of the window.

I don't want to know how big my student loan is. I never open mail from the IRD because I know what it will tell me. I have spent tens of thousands of dollars on the papers I finished, and at least $5000 on papers I didn't. Plus there was $1000 on course-related costs every year for four years, and $170 a week for living costs which wasn't even really enough to live on anyway.

My parents sometimes loan me money: $100 from Mum here, $200 from Dad there, another $300 from Mum again. Every year they write off the debt for Christmas, but one day I would like to pay them back.

My coworkers often cover my shifts when I'm sick. Usually I'm not sick; I'm hungover. I've promised to do the same for them, but I haven't yet.

Whenever it's my turn to buy toilet paper, I buy a four-pack. Everyone else in the flat buys eight-, twelve- or sixteen-packs.

I don't buy milk, but I drink milk. When I'm drunk, and I'm often drunk, the whole fridge is up for grabs. My flatmates have taken to storing their favourite foods in their rooms.

Mum paid for me to go to the dentist and to the optometrist. I lost my glasses after a couple of months and I've avoided talking to her since then so she doesn't find out.

Should I talk about Patrick? I don't want to talk about Patrick.

I bought my laptop on tick. I bought my phone on tick. I bought my camera on tick. I broke my laptop screen. I lost my phone on purpose so people couldn't call me. I spilled beer on my camera. I'm still paying all three off. It has been three months since I last made a payment.

My boss asked me to work late one weekend and I told him to go fuck himself. I haven't returned to work since then.

I don't know how I even got a credit card.

In my first year of university, my bank gave me a $1000 overdraft. I don't know where it went. The next year I needed the overdraft to pay bond. The next year I needed the overdraft to pay bond. The next year I needed the overdraft to pay bond. They did not give me an overdraft this year. I owe my flatmates $780 for bond. I owe the bank $4000. They are now charging interest.

Okay, I'll talk about Patrick. Every weekend between the ages of fourteen and nineteen, Patrick and I would get drunk together. I would spend the last of my money on beer, not eat dinner, and get absolutely wasted. To stop this Patrick would buy me a souvlaki and say, 'Make sure you pay me back this time.' I never paid him back.

Who in their right mind let me get a dog?

Last Christmas, I used my credit card to buy presents for my family to say thanks for putting up with me. I bought my father a fishing rod. I bought my brother a guitar. I bought my mother a sewing machine. I told them I had won some money on a scratchie. I bought myself a new stereo and a PlayStation. I have been buying scratchies since then to try and make the money back. All I have won is more scratchies.

I owe Patrick my life. He caught me drunk in the act, with my bad head and a knife and my arms in a bloody mess. He pulled me away and held me and didn't let go. I cried into his shoulder for twelve hours and bled all over his nice shirt.

'I owe you everything,' I said.

'You owe me nothing,' he said.

I don't return favours.

I have done bad things I've never told anyone about.

I have been paying off my debt to Work and Income at $10 a week for the past twenty-five weeks. I only have five weeks to go.

I've stopped smoking weed because I owe both my dealers $100 each. Word has gotten round and no one will sell to me anymore.

It's been two years since I last saw Patrick.

I sold my new PlayStation and stereo for rent money, but I didn't spend the money on rent. I don't know what I spent it on.

Debt collection agencies are sending me letters. I haven't opened any of them.

I owe the video store a copy of *Forrest Gump* on DVD. I wanted to return it but I kept forgetting it and then I threw it in the bin thinking it would go away. It hasn't.

I still haven't paid my share of last December's power bill.

I'm accumulating sleep debt.

I owe the university library $180 and they won't let me graduate until I pay it.

I owe countless people countless cigarettes.

I have benefited from colonisation and genocide and I don't even donate blood.

I owe my dog a nice long walk.

Last night I unlocked my door for the first time in weeks and packed my bag with a few changes of clothes and nothing else. I knelt down and rubbed my dog's head and let him lick my face and I left the house. I got to the supermarket ten minutes before it closed. I was going to spend the last of my money on a bottle of wine, but I bought a pack of gum instead and put the rest of it in the charity box. I walked north until the city got industrial, then suburban, then the yards got bigger and the footpath disappeared until I was walking by paddocks along the muddy grass next to the road. I chewed gum and kept walking until the paddocks turned back into suburbs and the footpath reappeared. I passed another supermarket, where I paused outside to spit my flavourless gum into the rubbish bin. Then I kept walking, past a McDonald's, a petrol station, a car yard, another supermarket and back into the suburbs. The houses thinned out again and I was back on the muddy grass next to the road. Cars drove past and one flashed its lights at me but didn't stop. I kept walking at a steady pace. It was paddocks for a long time until there was a petrol station and a fish and chip shop, then more houses, and then there was a café with a bench outside. I sat on the bench and hugged my backpack. I held my head up and watched the sky lighten. A car parked in front of me and two people and a greyhound got out. They unlocked the door to the café and went in. Twenty minutes later the people came back out of the café. One put a sign outside and the other latched the door open. They went back inside and a jogger ran past. The greyhound came out of the café and put her head on the bench next to me. I patted her and she looked at me. Her tail didn't wag. I stopped patting her and she kept looking at me so I patted her again.

'She likes you,' the café owner said from the doorway.

'Thanks,' I said.

'She's not bothering you, is she?' the café owner said.

'No, if anything she is not bothering me enough.' I patted the dog for a while longer and she looked right up at me the whole time. I didn't like looking in her eyes. Then, without warning, she turned around and went back into the café.

I sat on the bench looking across the road at a blue house. People came in and out of the café and the traffic got heavier. I pinched my arm as hard as I could and counted the seconds I could stand it: 119. I tried again with a different part of my arm and only lasted 94 seconds. I scrunched my eyes closed as tight as they would go and put my hands over my eyes to stop light coming in. I pushed the heels of my palms hard into my eyes and the black turned into flashing bright white. I stared at the white so hard it burned, until I could see through it to my nerves in the back of my eyes.

Someone called my name. I took my hands away from my eyes and the world was a shining white with black pulsing lines. A figure crossed the road towards me. He was silhouetted against bright white. His arms were stretched out, with rays of sunlight falling all around him. He was holding two souvlakis and had a smile on his face that looked like a million bucks.

2

2000ft ABOVE WORRY LEVEL

We hadn't spent much time with Georgie growing up but we were taking her on our annual camping trip because her parents needed some space, which I later learnt meant they were going to get divorced. She had a Walkman and a selection of tapes with all the best songs recorded off the radio. Half an hour into the trip she put her earbuds in. Because I was the smallest, I was made to sit in the middle.

Toby sat next to me with his arms crossed to hide the fact that he was constantly poking me in the side. I said 'Dad' out loud, but when I did Toby pinched me hard, which I knew meant if I narked I would pay for it later, so I asked how much longer the drive would be. Dad said we weren't even halfway. It would be another four or five hours. I put up with the poking for as long as I could, then I whacked Toby on the nose, and then he did the same back to me but harder. Dad swerved the car onto the side of the road. He didn't want to know who started it or for what reason, but I was moved to the side of the car and Georgie was put in the middle. I fell asleep after Ōamaru and when I woke up, once we turned inland at Palmerston, Toby had one of Georgie's earbuds in and they were nodding along in time with each other. Mum looked at Georgie and Toby through the mirror and said, 'You know what, those two could be twins.' They had the same dark hair parted in the middle and the same bored teenage expression on their faces. Toby was much taller than Georgie, even though she was three years older than him. As we entered Naseby we drove past a sign that said '2000ft. Above Worry Level!', but this was the summer that the village was infested with wasps.

Georgie was the first to get stung. We were setting up our tents and one flew into our campsite and stung her right on the elbow. Toby killed it with a rolled-up magazine. Then another wasp came along and went straight for her again. She squealed and crawled into her tent, which she hadn't even erected. Toby and I had to pass her tent poles through a tiny gap in the zip and set up her fly for her. She didn't come out until night had fallen. The wasps dogged Georgie that whole summer.

'Must be able to smell the blood in her knickers,' Dad said. I thought this meant she had a bleeding bum.

Mum was the second. She stood on one the next morning as she walked barefoot to the tap to fill up her water bottle. Dad went on a mission into Ranfurly and returned with jandals for us all to wear.

The campground apologised profusely, and although they wouldn't give refunds, they did their part by giving all the campers fly swats. Within a couple of days Toby's swat was confiscated by Dad because he kept hitting me with it across the calves. 'What? I saw a wasp,' he'd tell Dad. Toby became an expert in catching wasps with his bare hands. He usually got stung in the palm but he was tough and fast and didn't seem to care. Sometimes he wouldn't kill them and would throw them at me instead, but once they'd regained their balance they went straight for Georgie.

Exterminators were called, but they couldn't find and kill the wasp nests, which were deep in the surrounding bush, as quickly as the wasps were spawning. Every now and then, hundreds of wasps swarmed the swimming dam, uphill from the campground, and everyone would rush into the water and submerge themselves. I was eleven years old and was only stung once.

An initiative between the campground, council and local businesses saw the Naseby dairy set up a wasp rebate, where they gave kids 2¢ per dead wasp brought to them. They handed out Ziploc bags to all the kids who entered the store and set up special scales on the counter, next to the ice cream, to weigh the hauls. One hundred wasps weighed nine grams on average and would get you $2. Children wandered around the campground and forest in gangs, with their fly swats sticking out of the back of their shorts for quick access. There were always three or four kids crouched on the floor of the dairy counting out their dead wasps. Every now and then the teenagers would bum rush the store with beanies or stockings over their heads and scoop up handfuls of wasps, then bolt. The dairy tried to stop this by limiting the wasp rebate to children under twelve, but this just caused a black market to emerge.

'Psst,' the teenagers said to me one day. 'Two hundred and fifty wasps for $2.' They held up a Ziploc bag crammed with wasps above my head.

'Don't trust the teenagers, it's probably half full of bees and flies,' Dad told me later that day, when I asked him if I could borrow a couple of bucks and promised to at least double the investment.

My family's campsite dominated the campground, taking up most of the plateau at the top of the grounds. In the middle of our campsite we erected a big old marquee. The marquee originally belonged to Granddad, and Dad had taken it on every single camping trip he had ever been on. It was made of a thick green canvas and dated back to the War. The last time we'd gone camping we got caught in a storm and the marquee was ripped up all over. Mum said she wasn't going to sleep in it again, so we bought a bunch of smaller tents – a dome for Mum and Dad and three small pup tents for Toby, Georgie and me. Dad insisted on bringing the marquee anyway because it wouldn't feel like camping without it. He said we could use it as a lounge and he would get it fixed up and good as new over the holiday. He found a roll of canvas in the same shade of green as the tent and brought it with him, but when we unpacked the marquee we realised that over the years the tent had faded from a forest green to a much lighter green. It was only when you looked right up close at the stitching that you saw traces of the deep green that it used to be. The marquee was so heavy that not even Dad tried to carry it by himself, but that didn't stop Toby, who pulled it out from the trailer and held it in his arms. His face went red and he arched his back and his legs almost buckled with every step but he got it to the middle of our campsite on his own.

Dad set it up to house our chilly bins, deck chairs, bicycles and barbecue, and every morning we pulled up the front of it so Mum could sit in the shade reading magazines and looking out over the campground. Dad spent a good few hours a day repairing the marquee. He cut the new canvas he'd brought with him into patches with a Swiss Army knife, and hand-stitched it over the holes with a giant needle.

Everyone at the campground started calling our site Tent City, a name we embraced. Toby and I even painted a sign on a piece of the backup canvas that read 'You Are Now Entering

Tent City', complete with a drawing of our old marquee. We stuck it to the side of our van, which was parked up next to our site.

The day after we arrived, another family set up their campsite in the small patch of grass next to ours. They all slept in a single medium-sized tent and didn't take up much room. The family had a boy my age and he came into Tent City that evening and introduced himself to me. His name was Elliot.

'You've made a friend already,' Mum said after Elliot left. She made me invite Elliot around for breakfast the next morning. Elliot was skinny and had thick glasses that made his eyes look huge and a chest that looked like a birdcage. He had asthma and was allergic to bee stings but not wasp stings. Every time he heard buzzing he'd pause and hold his breath, and his eyes would dart around trying to identify the sound. Once he saw it was a wasp he'd breathe out and we'd pull our swats out of the back of our shorts and chase it down.

His mum showed me how to stab him with an EpiPen that he had to take everywhere he went in case he got stung. He carried this and his inhaler around in a backpack that was wider than he was. In the backpack he also kept his most cherished possession, a green drawstring purse made by his gran, which was filled with semi-precious stones he had got for every birthday and Christmas for the past few years. His little sister used to try to sneak a look at them when he wasn't around, so now he kept them with him everywhere he went. He also had a test tube filled with layers of different coloured sands he'd collected at Saint Bathans.

'Every colour comes from a different geological period,' Elliot told me. 'The lake weathered down different rocks at different times and if you dig you can find them all.'

Elliot was excited to be in Naseby because it used to be a gold-mining town, and he was keen to try some panning in some of the old sluicing sites. Dad gave us a couple of woks to use. We were allowed to have them all day, as long as we cleaned them and gave them back before he started making dinner. Every morning we strapped the woks to our backpacks and biked into the forest to pan in the water race. Dad told us if a swarm of wasps appeared while we were panning we should jump into the water and lie down, and if we were biking, bike in a straight line as fast as we could away from them.

Instead of hanging out with the other teenagers – who sulked around in a clearing in the forest near the caretaker's shed during the day, and snuck beers from their parents and lit bonfires at night, leaving behind piles of cigarette butts wherever they went – Toby and Georgie became the leaders of the kids. Toby was thirteen and was big for his age. He had just finished his last year of primary school where he was one of the prize sports stars, and was about to start high school. Before we left for Naseby, my dad took him shopping for his new uniform and told him, 'You better not bloody go through another spurt over summer.' Toby was already as tall as Dad and had fuzz on his upper lip. Georgie was sixteen but looked much younger. She'd seemed much older than Toby and me when we were younger, but at around thirteen she seemed to stop growing and we caught up with her. She was a quiet girl who did well at school and only had a handful of friends. Toby and Georgie told the rest of the campground they were twins and were fifteen years old. They wandered around the campground all day followed by an army of boys with fly swats sticking out of their shorts, killing and collecting in their Ziploc bags any wasp that dared to chase Georgie. I don't know if they followed her for love or money but she embraced the popular girl lifestyle wholeheartedly and was not stung again.

At night Toby and Georgie sat on the trampoline in the play area, surrounded by kids. Their favourites were allowed up on the tramp with them and the rejects had to sit on the bark or the swings, too far away to hear their stories of high school. Toby didn't even know what high school was like, but he was good enough at bluffing not to get caught out. I didn't want to risk losing my place on the tramp by calling out their lie. At home Toby made my life hell, but in Naseby I was by default third in command and was always allowed on the tramp. Elliot never was.

Toby and Georgie came up with a nickname for him a couple of days after we arrived. My family were at the swimming dam, sitting at the edge of the water applying sunscreen, when we heard a distant slapping sound coming up the dirt path. We turned and saw Elliot arriving, fully kitted out in a pair of flippers, goggles, Speedos and a snorkel, walking with great big steps, making clouds of dust with each one. I waved to him but he couldn't see me without his glasses, and when I called his name he jumped in surprise, tripped on one of his flippers and fell over.

'Check out Flip over there,' Georgie said and everyone laughed. I tried to avoid Elliot at the dam, which turned out to be easy. He swam with his head down and snorkel up, trying to see the river rocks at the bottom of the water, kicking his flippers and spraying everyone around him.

That night, as they did every now and then, the teenagers showed up at the trampoline. Their younger siblings vanished to the corners of the playground and watched silently as the teenagers tried to convince Georgie to drink beer with them in the forest.

One of the teenagers opened his jacket up to show three beer cans in the inside pockets. 'Come on Georgie,' he said. 'I nicked these from my dad and we're gonna drink them in the bush.'

Georgie yawned and said, barely looking at him, 'Maybe some other time.'

'Only three beers,' Toby scoffed.

The teenager took a pack of cigarettes out of his pocket and put one behind his ear. 'More than you've got, kid,' he said.

'You heard her, piss off,' Toby said, obviously offended that the invitation didn't extend to him.

Once the teenagers left, their younger siblings appeared back at the tramp and cheered the bravery of Toby and Georgie. For the next hour, there was a buzz of triumph in the air. Toby told an outlandish story of a non-existent party, straight from an American movie, complete with a pool in the backyard, spiked punch, and the cops showing up. Georgie corroborated the story, and all the kids were in awe. Elliot sat on the swings, too far away to hear the story, swinging back and forth by himself.

One day while we were out panning, Elliot told me about the traps his family set up around his yard to keep the bees away. 'You get a 1.5-litre bottle of cheap fizzy, raspberry works best because it has the most sugar, and you drink all but three to four centimetres of it. Then you cut the bottle in half, and turn the top half upside down and insert it into the bottom half. The bees fly in to get the drink and can't work out how to get out again.'

'Would it work for wasps?' I asked.

'Yeah, we get wasps in them all the time,' he said.

In that moment we gave up gold panning to become full-time wasp hunters. We biked down the hill to the Naseby dairy and cashed in our Ziploc bag full of wasps for the $3 needed to buy a 1.5-litre Budget raspberry fizzy. We drank it over the afternoon and set up the trap in the space between our campsites, where no other kids would see it. A couple of days later, we had enough wasps in the trap to pay for another bottle of fizzy, then a day later we bought a third. This invention was going to make us the richest kids in Naseby.

That night, high on sugar, Elliot brought his sleeping bag and Li-Lo into my pup tent and we stayed up all night talking about what we'd spend our money on. Elliot had his eye on more semi-precious stones. He took out his rock purse and showed me his collection. My favourite was obsidian, a jet-black rock, so smooth on one side it reflected the torchlight, with a sharp enough edge that it could cut you.

'Technically, it's not even a rock,' he said. 'It's volcanic glass.' He let me keep it, because he had more at home. 'It's not even that rare,' he said.

'It's cool that it's made in a volcano,' I said.

'Everyone thinks volcanic rocks are the best,' he said, 'but that's not even their real name, they're called igneous rocks. But they're not the coolest. The coolest types are metamorphic. Metamorphic rocks start out as sedimentary, and then deep in the Earth's crust, under immense heat and pressure, they transform into really tough strong metamorphic rocks. They are the coolest.' He handed me a long piece of shiny greenstone. 'This is pounamu,' he said. 'It's metamorphic. And it's so tough, much tougher than igneous rocks.'

The stone was hard and smooth and had clouds of darker green inside it. 'Where can I get some?' I asked.

'It only comes from the South Island, but you're not allowed to buy it for yourself, someone has to give it to you. My gran gave this to me. It's a taonga.'

'You have a gay old time with Flip last night?' Toby asked me the next morning over fried potatoes and baked beans.

'Toby,' Dad said, raising his voice.

'You know, like the Flintstones,' Toby said. Then he sang the Flintstones song, emphasising 'gay old time'. 'It means having a good time.'

'I know what it means,' Dad said.

After breakfast I returned Elliot's sleeping bag and Li-Lo to his campsite. 'I can't sleep when you're in my tent,' I told him and his family, 'so you can't stay over anymore.'

I spent the next three days trying to avoid Elliot. The first day was easy because my family went to Queenstown. Dad complained about the prices and we caught the gondola up the hill. We travelled back through the Central Otago countryside, stopping off to pick apples at an orchard in Cromwell, then we had the Sunday Roast Special at the Ranfurly Tavern. In Ranfurly I saw a sign in the window of the Four Square advertising Budget Soft Drink for 99¢.

The second day I told my family I felt sick, and stayed in my tent for an extra few hours until the heat became unbearable. I spent the rest of the morning hanging out at the back of the marquee looking through the chilly bins and annoying Mum. She gave me a special puzzle edition of *That's Life*, but I could only do the word-finds. Dad eventually took pity on me and took me to the Naseby museum, where he read every single piece of writing in every room, which took hours.

On the third day I followed Toby and Georgie through the

forest to an abandoned goldmine they said they had found. They told me they'd let me follow them as long as I kept it a secret. We had to shake off a bunch of younger kids who wanted to follow us by promising them a spot on the tramp later on. We walked for an hour around the path beside the water race before Georgie said we were nearly there. We jumped across the race, where it was at its most narrow, away from the track into the bush. Toby tied a hanky around my eyes and led me for five minutes then the two of them spun me around so I wouldn't be able to find where I was.

'Careful where you step,' Toby told me as he untied the hanky. 'There are mine shafts everywhere around here that go a hundred metres deep.'

At each footstep I tested the ground in front of me by putting a foot down and slowly putting my weight on it, and soon I was lagging behind Toby and Georgie. They confidently darted through the dense bush, around the trees, changing direction as they moved towards their goldmine until they were out of sight. Once they disappeared I stood still, terrified of taking steps in any direction, and unsure which way would lead me to the goldmine.

Then the buzzing started. I pulled my swat out from the back of my shorts and tried swatting the wasps away but there were too many. I yelled. I ran. I tried quickly testing each step as I ran, but it was slowing me down and the wasps kept appearing, so I just ran, terrified of falling down a shaft. I ran until I found the water race and jumped in. The race was shallow so I had to lay completely flat with only my mouth sticking out of the water to breathe. I heard some steps, then splashes and laughter. I looked up and Toby was throwing rocks into the race next to me. I got out of the race and hauled myself up onto the path.

'There were wasps,' I said, wringing the front of my T-shirt to get the water out.

'So what?' Toby said. 'There are wasps everywhere.' Then he uncurled his fist and threw one at me. It fell to the ground, dead.

'Why did you run off like that?' Georgie said. 'You missed the mine.'

'Did you find any gold?' I said.

'Nah,' Toby said. 'There was a bit of silver, but it's not worth our time.'

'Don't worry, we won't tell your mum and dad you ran off,' Georgie said.

The campground was only a ten-minute walk back from the path.

Toby told Dad I jumped in the water race because I thought I saw some gold. 'He's got gold fever,' he said.

'I do not, I know there's no gold here anymore.'

'I dunno. There might be a bit left,' Dad said. He offered us his woks again. 'Just in case you and Elliot want to give it another shot.'

I was made to go have a hot shower and by the time I got out Toby and Georgie had disappeared back into the forest. I checked the traps and they were getting full again. I sat in the marquee with Mum and read an old *That's Life*, but she took it off me when she saw me reading about a couple's sex life. 'It's not age-appropriate,' Mum said.

'Go and find Elliot,' Dad yelled from the behind the marquee where he was trying to sew a patch on. 'Take the woks.'

I wandered around the campground with the woks in hand, trying to avoid Elliot. I climbed up to the swimming dam and back down to the caretaker's shed, where I found myself surrounded by a group of teenagers.

'Hey, little bro,' one of them said. 'You're Georgie's brother right?' He stank of cigarettes.

'She's my cousin,' I said.

'Do you know where she is?'

'Sorry, I don't.'

'Tell her when you see her we're gonna light off some fireworks behind the dam tonight.'

It was still a couple of hours before tea so I went to the kitchen to see if the old TV there was playing cartoons. An old man was watching game shows and didn't look like he was going anywhere. Elliot was at the table with his little sister. He had all his semi-precious stones laid out in front of them.

'No, you can't have one,' Elliot was saying to her. 'You got your own stuff for Christmas, it's not my fault you wanted junk.'

His sister picked up a shiny red stone and dull blue stone and started smacking them together.

'Stop it, you'll scuff them,' he said. She let go of the blue stone and clenched her fist around the red one.

'Put it back,' he said.

'Put what back?' she said.

'I know you've got my jasper in your hand.'

She let the red stone go and wiped her arm across the table, sending all the rocks flying to the ground, and then she ran out of the kitchen.

I picked up a couple of the stones and put them on the table. 'Hey,' I said.

'Hey,' Elliot said. He was on his hands and knees picking up the rest of the stones off the ground.

'Have you checked the traps today?' I asked.

'Nah, not yet. Have you?'

'Yeah, there are heaps in there. Probably hundreds.'

'Cool.' He looked at the woks I had been carrying around. 'You going panning?'

'Nah, Dad just sent me to the kitchen to clean them,' I said. 'We could go tomorrow though?'

'Sounds good,' he said. 'I've been looking at the map and found a place where there used to be sluicing that might still have some gold.'

'Toby and Georgie found an abandoned goldmine in the forest,' I said. 'They said there wasn't any gold left but there might have been some silver.'

'Ha ha, I doubt it,' Elliot said. 'Silver has never been found in Naseby. And they didn't have mines here. It was all done in the rivers.'

'I should probably wash the woks now,' I said. Elliot followed me to the sink and picked up a tea towel. The woks were already clean, so I pretended to scrub them for five minutes to put on a show, before putting them on the dish rack. Elliot wiped them with the tea towel and put them on the table.

'I don't need to be back at camp for another half an hour,' I told him. 'Maybe we could watch TV for a while?' The old man had since left and we changed the channel to the cartoons.

We watched until Toby arrived in the kitchen an hour later. 'Sorry to cut in on your date Flip, but tea's ready.'

Elliot threw the remote at Toby. 'That's not my name,' he yelled.

Toby caught it and placed it calmly on the table. 'That's not the point right now. The point is that dinner is ready and we need to take your boyfriend away.'

It was Toby's and my job to pull the deck chairs out of the marquee for dinnertime. Mum called it 'setting the table' and laughed every time she said it. Georgie was in her tent, avoiding the wasp that had been hanging round the site. Dad served up the sausages and fried potatoes on plastic plates. Mum started to spoon old supermarket coleslaw onto the sides, left over from our picnic in Queenstown, but Dad stopped her and made Toby and me do it ourselves. 'It's her holiday, not yours,' he said. 'We would have had veggies too, but someone took our woks away. Maybe you do have gold fever.'

'We didn't even go panning,' I said. 'I was in the kitchen the whole time.'

'That Flip has a temper on him,' Toby said. 'He better get that under control before you get married.'

'Toby,' Dad said, raising his voice.

'I didn't say they were getting married to each other, I just said "you". Anyway there's nothing wrong with being gay, are you a homophobe Dad?'

Dad pulled out his swat and whacked Toby around the calves. 'What? I saw a wasp,' he said.

Mum wouldn't let Georgie eat her dinner in her tent, so she ate her dinner with one hand waving her swat around.

'Those traps of theirs are attracting more wasps,' she said, waving her swat at me. 'Tell them to put them further away.'

I had to move our traps out from behind our campsite to the other side of the van, where they were in plain sight.

After dinner, the dishes were stacked in a bucket and given to Toby, Georgie and me to wash. Kids streamed out of their campsites to follow us as we walked to the kitchen. As soon as we were out of sight of Mum and Dad, the bucket was handed to a pair of keen children. Boys charged ahead, swiping left and right at the air. It was evening, so most of the wasps had disappeared, but the boys pretended anyway so that Georgie would be safe. By the time we arrived at the kitchen, the sink had already been filled and Toby and Georgie sat at the table and let the others do all the dishes. I stacked them back in the bucket, and Toby and Georgie refused help from enthusiastic kids who wanted to carry them back to our campsite. They told them to wait at the playground.

Other kids had already started to congregate there, waiting for the twins to arrive after they had returned the dishes. We could see them from the kitchen window. Elliot was there too. He was jumping alone on the tramp, ignoring all the pleas to get off so it would be ready for the twins to take their position. He hadn't even taken his backpack off and it was bucking up and down with him, slightly delayed.

'Do a flip,' Georgie yelled as we left the kitchen, and everyone laughed. Elliot did the fingers at us and kept bouncing.

We returned the dishes and came back to the playground, and Elliot was still bouncing insistently.

'Get off,' kids were yelling. They were throwing bark at him. But Elliot kept bouncing. Toby climbed up onto the tramp and sat in his usual position, right in the middle, but Elliot didn't stop.

'Come on Elliot,' I pleaded, 'let's go do something else.' I didn't want to do anything else. I wanted to sit up on the tramp next to Toby and Georgie. Elliot didn't respond. He kept bouncing.

Toby got up and started bouncing too. Other kids jumped onto the tramp and started bouncing. The trampoline creaked.

'Max two! Max two!' Elliot yelled, pointing at a sign on the side of the tramp. The kids kept bouncing. Toby kept bouncing. Elliot kept bouncing.

Georgie sat on a swing and pretended not to watch. A few boys wandered over to her and sat down, but most stayed and watched the action on the trampoline.

'All right, get off,' Toby said. He stopped bouncing and shooed all the kids off the tramp. 'We're done here now.' Elliot kept bouncing. Toby stood there glaring at Elliot, and then he took his shirt off.

The kids all gasped. 'Oooooooh.' Elliot kept bouncing. 'It's about to get real, Flip,' Toby said, and he did a big jump.

They bounced in unison, eyeballing each other. They got higher and higher with every bounce. Toby cracked a smile and started bouncing harder and faster, out of sync with their rhythm. Elliot started to lose his balance. Toby did one giant jump, landing a split second before Elliot did, and when Elliot hit the tramp he went flying, his body twisting in the air with his feet above his head. His glasses flew off his face and hit the ground, then Elliot did. Everyone was silent for about three seconds, and then Elliot started crying.

'Come on Flip, it's not that bad,' Toby said. 'You'll be all right.' He climbed off the tramp.

Elliot stood up. Both his knees and the palm of one of his hands were bleeding. I picked up his glasses. Elliot's sobs turned into wheezes. He took his inhaler out of his bag and sucked into it and both the wheezing and the sobbing stopped. I put his arm over my shoulder but he pushed it off straight away and hobbled towards our campsites.

'Dad's gonna be pissed,' I said to Toby and ran to catch up with Elliot.

Elliot's parents were at the Naseby pub, so Mum got out the first-aid kit. 'What happened?' she asked. Toby sulked around the edge of the campsite by the sign for Tent City.

'Toby bounced Elliot –' I started.

'I fell off the tramp,' Elliot said.

'What did Toby do?' Dad asked.

'Nothing, we were bouncing and I fell off,' Elliot said.

'This will sting a bit,' Mum said as she rubbed Dettol into

his knee. Elliot sniffed but didn't wince.

'Toby, what happened here?' Dad asked.

'Nothing happened. I just fell off,' Elliot said.

'It was an accident,' Toby said. 'We were jumping and he got too excited.'

Elliot sniffed.

'It doesn't sound like it was an accident, it sounds like it was an incident,' Dad said. 'An accident is when something happens outside your control –'

'– and an incident is when you are doing something you know could cause a problem, and you keep doing it anyway,' Toby finished.

'It was an accident,' Elliot said.

'Okay. I don't want to hear about any more accidents,' Dad said.

Mum put bandages on Elliot's knees and a big plaster on his palm and sent us off.

Toby and Elliot were sent away. Dad pulled me aside and said, 'Make sure you let me know if Toby's causing Elliot any grief.'

I caught up with Toby and Elliot. 'You're a pretty tough kid,' Toby was saying. Behind them, I kicked at the bark on the path and looked at Elliot's giant backpack. He could completely fit inside it if he wanted to.

Back at the playground, kids were bouncing on the trampoline. When Toby took his position in the middle, the bouncing kids slowed down but didn't stop completely.

'Where's Georgie?' he asked them. A couple of the kids sat down, and another couple got off the tramp.

'Went off with the teenagers,' one of the kids finally said.

Toby was silent. Elliot climbed up, and Toby didn't even object. The kids started to slide away from him and disperse, uninterested in the lone twin.

'I'm gonna go find her,' he said. He wandered down towards the caretaker's shed where the teenagers usually hung out. After a while, Elliot and I followed him.

At the shed, Toby was sitting on a tree stump surrounded by cigarette butts and a single empty beer can.

'I think they're up behind the swimming dam,' I said.

'I don't even care where she is,' Toby said.

'We brought our Monopoly set, do you want to go play that?' Elliot said.

Toby got off the stump and headed uphill in the direction of the swimming dam. Elliot and I followed him. The path was dark and hard to navigate but Toby walked on determinedly. We started hearing pops and crackles in the distance, and as we reached the top of the path we saw the glow of faces illuminated by sparklers on the far side of the dam.

To get to the far side you had to either swim across the dam or walk through the bush. We walked through the bush. Toby was silent but fast. Elliot started murmuring. I punched him on the arm and he shut up. Other than the occasional sparkle through the trees, it was black. Ahead of us, Toby stopped at the edge of the clearing. We caught up and stood behind him.

Some of the boys were shirtless and looked like they had been swimming. Georgie was sitting on a log beside another girl and casually holding a sparkler.

'What are you going to do, Toby?' Elliot whispered. Toby shushed him. A boy turned and saw us, the one I had talked to earlier that day.

'Good one, Flip,' I said under my breath.

'Hey, little bros,' the teenager said. 'Welcome to our party.'

'This is barely a party,' Toby said.

The teenager shrugged and took a sip of beer. 'What do you

know about parties, kid.'

Georgie came over. Her face was illuminated by the sparkler she was holding. 'Hey Toooooby,' she said. 'Everything okay with you, Elliot? Spectacular flip you did earlier.'

'I'm fine,' Elliot said.

Something buzzed around my head. The wasps had normally disappeared by night time, but the occasional one hung around. Elliot froze and his eyes darted, but it was impossible to make anything out in the blackness. Toby lunged forward and closed his fist around the buzz. The teenager jumped back. 'Whoa, what are you doing little bro?'

Toby whipped his arm forward and opened his fist. The wasp landed on the teenager's cheek. 'What the hell,' he yelled. Georgie's sparkler went out. There were screams, then we were running. Through the bush, down the path, across the campground, past the kitchen, past the playground, back to our campsite. We ran on instinct, without looking, without tripping. We were back at camp in minutes. Toby was first back, Elliot was second; he was faster than I thought and he ran through the trees confidently with his backpack bobbing up and down. By the time I arrived back at camp he was already sucking on his inhaler.

We puffed and laughed until a 'Shhh' came out of Mum and Dad's tent. Elliot and I checked the wasp traps by torchlight and there were hundreds of them. We were rich. We agreed that the next morning, instead of panning, we would bike down to the dairy and cash in. We laughed maniacally until Elliot's mum yelled for us to shut up and for him to get to bed. Elliot crawled into his tent and Toby and I sat on the deckchairs in the marquee, catching our breath and laughing quietly.

Georgie opened the marquee flap soon after. 'Oh my God,

Toby, that wasp stung Jack three times. He's got welts all over his face.'

Toby laughed. Another 'Shhh' came out of Mum and Dad's tent, so we all went to bed. The adrenaline was still pumping but I scrunched my eyes closed and made myself sleep, because in the morning I would be rich.

I woke to the sound of our marquee falling over and Toby swearing loudly. I crawled out of my tent and shone my torch at Toby who was jumping up and down saying swear words. He was covered in wasps.

'What the hell is happening,' Dad said. He climbed out of his tent, pulling a T-shirt over his chest. 'What have you done, Toby?' He lifted up one side of the marquee, which was on a heap on the ground, and tried to erect the pole in the middle of it, but the guy ropes had been cut and it wouldn't stay up.

'I didn't do anything,' Toby said. 'Someone opened my tent and threw wasps all over me.'

Shit. I ran to the van and saw that the traps were gone. The sign on our van had been tagged and now read, 'You Are Now Entering Tent SHity' and the marquee had been scribbled over with a drawing of a poo.

'Toby, I don't care who you piss off as long as you keep them away from our campsite,' Dad said.

I tried picking up the wasps from around Toby's tent. Most of them were dead, but some were hazy and crawling around. I put as many as I could find in my Ziploc bag, but Dad told me to go back to sleep and deal with it in the morning.

The next morning Elliot woke me up by shaking my tent. 'The traps are gone,' he hissed. I got up and told him what had happened, and we got on our hands and knees and searched around Toby's tent for any remaining wasps. We pulled some deck chairs out of the fallen marquee and waited for what seemed like hours for Toby to get up. Then we searched his tent for wasps. But we only found another twenty or so.

There were only around fifty all up, after we'd given up counting. Fifty wouldn't even buy us a single new bottle for another trap. We'd lost hundreds of wasps, and dollars of cash.

Elliot had breakfast with us, baked beans on stale bread, and Toby dabbed ointment on all his new wasp stings. Dad offered us the woks in sympathy. 'Maybe you'll get lucky panning today?' he said.

Elliot fetched a map from his backpack and showed me a small offshoot of the water race in a far corner of the forest. 'Maybe there will be some gold here,' he said in a monotone. We both knew we wouldn't find any gold.

We pushed our bikes through the campsite, a wok strapped to each of our backpacks. If Elliot had just got off the tramp yesterday, when he should have, this never would have happened.

We came to the caretaker's shed, where the teenagers were hanging out.

'Oi, little bros,' one of them called. He had three welts on one of his cheeks. 'I've got three hundred wasps here, I'll give them to you for a special price of $3.' He held up Ziploc bag, chockablock full of wasps. I could see raspberry fizzy pooling in a corner.

'Those are our wasps,' Elliot said. 'You stole them from us.'

'Calm down, little dude,' the teenager said. 'We caught these wasps fair and square.'

'You stole them from us, and threw them on Toby.'

'I don't even know who Toby is,' he said. He turned to the teens behind him. 'Do you guys know who Toby is?'

'No idea,' they replied. 'Who's Toby?'

'We haven't got any money, but they're our wasps,' Elliot said.

'Tell you what. We'll give you the wasps, and you give us the money tomorrow. But you have to give us some collateral.'

I pulled Elliot aside. 'We could give them your stones. You'll get them back tomorrow.'

'No way,' he said.

'Come on Flip. If you had just got off the tramp yesterday, we wouldn't be in this mess.'

'Uuuuh,' he said.

'We'll go to the dairy, cash them in, and we'll have more than enough to buy another trap and pay them back. You'll have them back by the end of the day.'

We turned back to the teenagers.

'How about these,' Elliot said to them, holding up his bag of stones.

The first teenager took them off him, opened the drawstring and said, 'Yep, okay. You bring us $3 by the end of tomorrow and you'll get your rocks back.'

'Be careful with them,' Elliot said. 'And I know exactly what's in there so don't try stealing any.'

The teenager handed over the bag of wasps. They smelled like raspberry.

With the three hundred from the teenagers, and the fifty we collected from around Toby's tent, we had $7 worth of wasps. That was enough to buy us a bottle of raspberry for a new trap, pay back the teenagers, and have a dollar left over. We only had a week left in Naseby, and these were not the riches Elliot and I had dreamed of returning home with.

So I came up with a plan: we'd cash in the wasps and bike

to Ranfurly, where we could get three times as many bottles for our wasp rebate. With three traps going, we could catch back almost as many wasps as we lost. We had all day, and Ranfurly was only fourteen kilometres away.

We dumped the woks in a cupboard in the kitchen and biked down the hill to the dairy. As long as we were back at the campsite with the woks clean before dinner, no one would ask questions.

'How many wasps are here?' the dairy owner asked, holding our two Ziploc bags up to the light.

'Four hundred,' we said in unison. There were only three hundred and fifty, but we'd learnt to overestimate.

'Looks to me more like three hundred, maybe three-fifty if you're lucky,' he said, and emptied the bags into a sieve above a bin. Kids had been trying to artificially increase the wasp load by putting sand or small stones in with them, so the sieve had been introduced. Some kids even tried soaking their wasps in water to make them heavier, but wasps aren't very absorbent, so it didn't help much.

The dairy owner flicked the wasps around in the sieve and picked out a quite a few flies that had made their way into the bags. 'You've got some flies in here,' he said. 'You trying to trick me?'

'No,' I said. 'It's an accident, I promise.' I swore under my breath at the teenagers, who must have put them in there.

'You're meant to pick them out before you bring them here,' he said. He dumped the sieved wasps onto the scales. Thirty-one grams, the weight of roughly three hundred and fifty wasps. 'I'll give you five for them,' he said.

'Come on,' I said. 'There's way more than two hundred and fifty wasps there.'

'That's not fair,' Elliot said. 'The scales say there are three hundred and fifty. That's $7.'

'I don't have to buy them, you know. You can see if anyone else wants to buy three hundred dead wasps.'

'Fine. We'll take five,' I said. It was barely enough to cover our debt to the teenagers.

The dairy owner cracked a smile. 'I'll tell you what, let's split the difference. I'll give you six, but you're lucky this time. Whaddaya want? Lollies? Fizzy? Ice cream?'

'Cash,' Elliot said.

'What are you gonna do with cash?' the dairy owner asked. 'Cash won't rot your teeth.'

'We're gonna go down –' Elliot started.

'We're gonna come back tomorrow,' I interrupted. 'We're going out for dinner tonight and don't want to spoil our appetites.'

'First time I've heard kids say that. You sure you're under twelve? Can I see some ID?' He laughed and opened the till. He handed Elliot three shiny $2 coins. I took the coins from Elliot and pocketed them.

'See you tomorrow,' I said.

The road from Naseby to Ranfurly is fourteen kilometres and all downhill. It descends four hundred feet. You barely have to pedal biking it, but we did. I pedalled really hard, and was going so fast that my bike started shaking and my legs couldn't push quickly enough to keep up with the pedals. So I coasted, and looked behind me to see Elliot in the distance, pushing as hard as he could to catch up. His bike was cheap and the wheels were wonky. When he was just about to catch up, I started pedalling again, pulled ahead and yelled 'Hurry up Flip.'

I arrived at the Four Square a good three or four minutes before Elliot. He was puffing, and dirt from the road stuck to the sweat on his face. He pulled his inhaler out of his bag and puffed on it.

Neither of us had a lock, so I made Elliot look after the bikes while I went in and got the drinks. They were in the first aisle, stacked high, boxes and boxes with their fronts half cut off to display the bottles. I put three bottles of raspberry fizzy in my basket. It was heavy but manageable. I thought for a moment and put another three on top. The basket was heavier than I expected, but between the two of us it should be okay.

I paid with the three $2 coins and stepped outside. I put three bottles in my backpack and three in Elliot's.

'Why did you buy six?' Elliot asked. 'We've got to pay back the teenagers.'

'We've got till tomorrow to get $3. We'll get that easy with six traps,' I said. 'We'll go back to the dairy, get the money, pay them back and get back your precious stones.'

'Semi-precious stones,' Elliot corrected me. He held his bag up. 'I don't know if I'll be able to carry this many,' he said, 'and I'm thirsty.' We leaned against the Four Square and Elliot cracked open one of the bottles. It fizzed up and spilled out. He held the bottle away from him, letting the red drink spill on the footpath. As the sound of fizzing subsided, it was replaced with a low buzz. I had learned to love that buzzing sound. I looked around and saw a yellow and black blur. Elliot froze.

'I bet the wasps are all over Ranfurly too,' I told him. I swiped at the blur but missed. It flew about a metre away then turned around and went straight for Elliot.

'It's a bee!' he yelled, and crouched down with his hands over his head. He dropped the bottle on the ground. I went for another swipe and this time hit it. The bee was knocked sideways, but it got its balance back and went straight towards the fizzy that was spilling out of the bottle, right next to Elliot. He yelled.

I swiped again, but this time I closed my hand around it. It stung me as I crushed it in my palm. 'Got it,' I yelled.

Elliot stayed frozen. 'Was it the only one?'

We listened for more buzzing but couldn't hear any. I put the bee in my pocket. I picked up the bottle; it had about three centimetres of raspberry fizzy left, just enough for a wasp trap. I screwed the lid tight and put it back in Elliot's bag.

'Come on Flip,' I said, picking up my bike. I looked up at the sun. 'We gotta get back before tea.'

Elliot got up off the ground and picked up his bike. He had raspberry fizzy all over his pants. He looked around to see if there were any more bees before stepping on the pedal and lifting his leg over the frame.

We biked across the Ranfurly township, feeling the weight of the fizzy on our shoulders. We had to wait for ages at the intersection for the traffic to ease up enough for us to cross back onto the main road.

The road from Ranfurly to Naseby is fourteen kilometres and all uphill. It climbs four hundred feet. With four and a half kilos of fizzy in my bag, the journey was harder than I expected. Within five minutes Elliot needed a break. He was wheezing and the weight of his backpack was too much, even though most of one of his bottles had gone down the drain.

We stopped and cracked open another one of his fizzies and he sucked on his inhaler. We poured the fizzy into our mouths from a centimetre away so we wouldn't touch the same bit of the bottle with our lips.

'I don't think I can keep going,' he said. 'Let's tip out the drink.'

'We've already wasted one,' I said. I took his backpack and

strapped it to my front. I was carrying at least seven kilos of raspberry fizzy. We took off again.

Soon after we got back on the road, a big dusty truck flew past and covered us in dirt. The dirt stuck to the patches of raspberry we had spilled around our mouths, and all over Elliot's pants. Elliot started wheezing again. The road got steeper.

'Hurry up Flip,' I yelled as he slowed down. 'We can't stop now.' My legs were jelly and I knew if I stopped I wouldn't be able to start again. 'We've got to get back to the campsite. No one knows we're here.'

Elliot kept slowing down, and I kept looking back as he got further and further away. I saw him pull over. He let his bike fall to the ground and he stumbled off it and into a patch of grass. I had his backpack strapped to my front with his inhaler in it.

'Come on Flip,' I yelled from a distance. 'We're nearly halfway.' I don't think he heard me. He was doubled over and his torso was shaking. We were not nearly halfway.

A line of white vans came down the hill. About ten in a row, each with one driver. Elliot waved at them from the side of the road. The final white van did a U-turn and pulled over to the grass in front of Elliot. I stopped and watched for a bit, then turned around and went back to him. 'Why didn't you stop?' he tried to yell at me but he was wheezing so much I could barely make it out. I reached into the front pocket of his bag and gave him his inhaler.

The window of the van rolled down. A man in brown overalls was in the driver's seat. 'What are you boys doing all the way out here?' he said.

'We were heading back to Naseby,' I said. 'But Elliot got tired.'

Elliot wheezed.

'I was just up there,' he said. 'Chuck your bikes in the back, I'll get you back there.' He climbed out of the van and opened the boot. I lifted my bike up and slid it into the back. Elliot's hands were shaking and he couldn't even hold his bike upright.

'Jeez, are you okay kid?' the man said to Elliot. 'Do you need to go to the hospital?'

'I'm fine,' Elliot managed to say. 'We just have to get back to Naseby.'

The man lifted Elliot's bike into the van and put it on top of mine. There were no seats in the back of the van so Elliot and I shared the seat up front. I pulled the safety belt around both of us.

'Are you camping up in Naseby,' the man said. 'It's been a hell of a year for it, with the wasps.'

'It's been fun,' I said. 'We've been hunting them.'

'That's what I do for a job,' he said. 'We just spent the day in the bush. I reckon we've got them all.' Elliot took another puff of his inhaler. We were silent for the rest of the drive.

'Are you sure you don't want me to come in,' the man said, as he pulled up at the campground entrance.

'No,' Elliot said. 'Here's fine.'

I pulled both bikes out of the back. The chain had come off Elliot's so we had to wheel our bikes back through the campground. The first thing we noticed was that the campground felt empty. It looked like half the campsites had packed up and left that day. The second thing we noticed was the absence of the background buzzing that had been present all summer. I saw a dying wasp crawling along the ground. I stood on it and then picked it up and put into the Ziploc bag I had in my pocket. Then I saw another dying wasp and

103

I did the same. Elliot dropped to his knees and together we picked up wasp after wasp. There were dozens of them all over the ground. We must have picked up thirty or forty before someone interrupted us.

'Haven't you heard.'

We looked up. It was one of the boys who had been following Georgie. 'It's over,' he said.

'What do you mean it's over?' I said.

'The dairy isn't buying wasps anymore.'

'They can't do that,' I said. 'We had a deal.'

Elliot had dropped his wasps on the ground and was already wheeling his bike away. I followed him at a distance, stopping at a rubbish bin to throw my Ziploc bag away.

Toby was at the campsite by himself. He was tying together pieces of guy ropes. Mum and Dad had gone for the day and they'd told him he had to fix the marquee by the time they were back.

'Where's Georgie?' I asked.

'Gone off with the teenagers,' he said. He looked at Elliot. 'Shit. What happened to you?'

'Do I look that bad?' Elliot said.

'No. You look fine,' I said.

I took the bottles of fizzy out of my bag and drank from one of them, then handed it to Elliot.

'Where'd you get all that from?' Toby said.

Elliot told him about our deal with the teenagers and said I was an idiot and I'd spent all our money on fizzy and now we wouldn't be able to get his stones back.

'We'll get your stones back, Elliot,' Toby said. He pulled at two pieces of rope that he'd been trying to tie together. The knot held for a while but then fell apart. Toby took Dad's Swiss Army knife and we headed to the teenagers' area. Toby practised swinging the knife around on the way.

Georgie was sitting on the tree stump. There were only three teenagers left, all boys. 'Back already?' the lead teenager said. He had a Band-Aid on his face.

'Come on,' Toby said. 'It's me you want. Leave the kids out of this.'

'I have no interest in you whatsoever,' he said.

'What did you do to the kids, Jack?' Georgie said.

'We just did a little business deal.' He pulled the drawstring of stones out of pocket and threw it up in the air and caught it again.

'That's pathetic,' Georgie said. 'Give Elliot his stones back.'

'We had a deal,' Jack said. 'I'll give them back when they give us our money.' He opened the drawstring and pulled out a cloudy white stone and flicked it at Elliot's feet. 'You can have this one for free.' Elliot crouched to retrieve it and polished it on his T-shirt.

'How much do you want for them,' Georgie said.

'$10 now,' he said. 'I'm charging interest.'

'Give them back or else,' Elliot yelled.

Everyone laughed, even Toby and Georgie. Elliot looked furious. I stood next to him, holding a bottle of fizzy like a club.

'Great weapon you've got there,' Jack said. He pulled another stone out of the drawstring bag. It was the pounamu. Elliot screamed. I shook up the bottle and undid the lid a little bit and then threw it towards Jack. The lid came off and raspberry fizzy sprayed everywhere. Jack dropped the pounamu and Elliot dived for it. Georgie reached for the bag of stones in the chaos but Jack closed his hand over it and pushed her away. Georgie tripped over and fell backwards into the tree stump.

Toby charged at Jack with the Swiss Army knife. The two other teenagers tackled him and held him down on the ground. They pulled the knife from him easily and threw it away into the bush. I only realised then how much bigger they were than him. I jumped on top of one of the teenagers and grabbed handfuls of his hair. He turned to me and held me down and I kicked and punched and yelled but he was too big.

Georgie yelled, 'Let him go, he's just a kid.'

I looked around for Elliot but he wasn't there, and I realised Georgie was talking about me. I hoped Elliot hadn't gone to get an adult.

Georgie tried to kick Jack, but Jack grabbed her foot and pushed it back down to the ground. Toby managed to get out from under the other teenagers and ran to Jack. Jack swung his hand around, and the bag of stones connected with Toby's face. Toby didn't even flinch, and swung back at him, connecting his fist with Jack's nose. Jack swung again, but Georgie had jumped up onto his back and had her hands around his neck. Her hands were tiny, probably smaller than mine, and her fingers thin. They weren't doing much. She dug her fingernails in and he started spinning around trying to get her off. He dropped the bag of stones on the ground. I kicked and kicked until the teenager got off me and I went to get the stones, but by the time I had got to them they had already been picked up. Jack managed to pull Georgie's arms off his neck and pushed her onto the ground. He stood over her, but before he could do anything else Elliot appeared behind him. Elliot jumped up and his hand flashed at Jack's neck. Jack instantly dropped to his knees. He clutched his neck and started heaving. Elliot stood over him. He was holding his EpiPen in one hand like a dagger and his bag of semi-precious stones in the other, and was wearing his backpack that he could probably fit into if he wanted to.

SANTA, THE CHRISTMAS HEDGEHOG

On Christmas Day a huge hedgehog fell down a drain next to the house. The drain was the size of a decent bucket, and the hedgehog took up the whole thing. It was the biggest hedgehog any of us had ever seen. Mum had been telling Dad for years to cover up the drain because every time she walked down that side of the house she'd almost fall into it. It wasn't even a working drain – it was from before we fixed up the plumbing. It was half filled with gravel and about a foot and a half deep.

We asked Dad and Uncle Ed, who had brought his new wife and an army of little kids around, what we should do, and Dad said, 'I suppose we should get him out of there.'

It took a long time to get Santa – we called him Santa – out of the drain. He curled up whenever we touched him, and he was so big and heavy and prickly that it wasn't just a matter of picking him up from the top. You had to get your hands right under him, which Santa wasn't making easy. Toby somehow managed to lift him up on the side, slide a dustpan underneath him and pull him out. Mum told Toby to put him down in the backyard. On the way there, Toby, being Toby, kept on pretending to trip up or drop him, swinging his arms wildly, stumbling around to the left and right, going, 'Whoa, whoa, whoa.'

Mum followed him, yelling, 'Careful! Careful!', her voice getting higher and higher every time Toby stumbled. Santa was hanging half off the side of the dustpan, not because Toby wasn't being careful, but because Santa was so fat.

Toby got Santa to the backyard safe and sound, and we put him down at the bottom of the garden. Mum gave Toby a smack around the back of the head and said he nearly gave her a heart attack. We locked the dog round the front so Santa would have time to get his bearings without being too disturbed. But after an hour he hadn't moved so Toby put him on the dustpan again and we put him in a basket in the spare room. We gave him a blanket and some cat biscuits and he ate them and snuffled around a bit.

Dad told us to leave Santa alone and Uncle Ed's new wife told us to let him sleep. She told us hedgehogs were nocturnal so we'd release him into the garden once night came. So we had tea, and messed around. Dad and Uncle Ed got a bit pissed and Mum asked us to please not drown all our food in tomato sauce, especially not the potato salad. She said this was the last year she was going to put so much effort in, and next year we would just have barbecued pre-cooks and supermarket coleslaw and packets of chips. And that was all right with us of course; the sausages and chips were our favourite part of the tea anyway. Mum sighed and said, 'Why do I even bother?'

We ate a dessert of pavlova and scoops of ice cream and instant pudding, while watching the sky and waiting for the sun to set. After it disappeared out of sight over the houses across the road, we crowded Dad and asked if we could check on Santa. Dad looked at the sky, which was still light, and said, 'Ah, all right then.' We rushed into the spare room and there

Santa was, in the basket. He'd eaten most of the cat biscuits and given birth: four little things, smaller than mice, with white translucent spikes and pink skin, lying there dead.

The little kids asked what was happening, and why the baby hedgehogs weren't moving. Toby gathered the kids in a semi-circle in front of him, got down on one knee and said, 'This is what happens sometimes, sometimes things die and that's just part of life.' Mum put her hand on Toby's shoulder and nodded. 'And besides,' Toby said, 'the hedgehog couldn't be called Santa, because she was a girl, so her name must be Mary, and one of these baby hedgehogs was the hedgehog Jesus.' Mum took her hand off Toby's shoulder and prodded his arm. Toby continued, 'This hedgehog Jesus was going to come back alive in a couple of days and save all of the hedgehogs of the world.'

'That's quite enough,' Mum said. She yanked Toby to his feet by the armpit, but by then everyone was squealing and dancing around the room.

'All hail our hedgehog lord and saviour,' Toby yelled, and whooped, and the kids whooped along too.

Mum yelled at Toby to piss off to his room, and that Dad had better fill that bloody drain in tomorrow. Dad had to tell the kids that Toby was joking and the babies were going to stay dead. The kids stopped dancing and whooping.

Dad dug a shallow grave in the backyard, near where the rabbits were buried, and we had a wee funeral for the baby hedgehogs. Mum suggested we sing a song, but the only one the little kids knew was 'Rudolph the Red-Nosed Reindeer', because they don't teach proper carols in school anymore, so we sang that. Then we had to call Toby back from his room because he was the only one who could do the thing with the dustpan.

HOME

I got kicked out of my flat and fired from my job. Mum had just bought a new house in her old hometown so I suggested to her that I could come stay for a while and help set it up. I deactivated my Facebook account and bought a plane ticket.

The only flatmate with any sympathy left for me asked if I was excited to move home.

'It isn't home. It's where my mum lives. I've never lived there before,' I said.

'Home is where your mum is,' my flatmate said.

'Home is where your stuff is,' I said. I had left most my stuff outside the Salvation Army.

A few years ago Mum and Dad did dance classes together. It was pretty cute. I had never – and still have never – seen Dad do anything that resembled dancing, but every Wednesday night for a year they would go off to a school hall in the next suburb over and learn the basics of waltz and foxtrot and those kinds of things.

'Oh, it's all just a bit of fun,' Mum said. 'We're not taking it seriously.'

After a year, Dad decided it wasn't for him anymore. They stopped going out and Dad got very into the news. Every night after the six o'clock news he would watch the other channel's timeshifted six o'clock news, and after that he'd change to an international news channel.

Whenever Toby and I went home for dinner Dad would tell us about another violent attack that had happened somewhere in the country, or in another country like ours. Sometimes they were random and sometimes they were part of a pattern unfolding.

'I honestly believe we are heading for a war,' Dad said. 'It's happening locally, it's happening nationally, it's happening internationally. People are not respecting each other. Not respecting authority. Something is brewing.'

Mum watched with him for a while, but complained that they paid for all those channels and only ever ended up watching three of them. She bought a second TV for the bedroom – something she'd never allowed when we were growing up. 'What kind of house needs two TVs?' she used to say.

Eventually Mum got bored of TV and went back to the dance class alone. Within a month she had graduated to the advanced class. Every time she came home Dad would ask her who she'd danced with that week.

'Sometimes she has to dance with the other women,' Dad told me at a family dinner. He laughed. Mum stayed quiet.

Dad took over the laptop. He'd sit on the sofa hunched over the coffee table, browsing news websites while the news played on TV. He would sit down straight after work and stay there until after the table had been set for dinner, then return to the laptop straight after dessert. Mum kept a notebook of things to research: books people had recommended to her, auctions for box sets of TV shows she used to love, articles her co-workers were talking about. Whenever Mum finally got to use the laptop, she would pull out her notebook and get a week's worth of internet out of the way in an hour. When Mum was using the laptop, Dad wouldn't look at the screen or read over her shoulder, but would sit close by, waiting to have it back.

Toby bought Mum a smartphone for Christmas so she could use the internet without having to wait her turn. Every time Toby or I came around we would have to show her how to use it again – which button was the camera and where the photos were saved and how to attach them to an email if she wanted to send them to us. Mum got sick of asking us for help, so she enrolled in a class called Communicating through Technology. She told us about learning how to make and edit short videos using an app. She said it was amazing what you could do on a tiny machine.

'Why do you even need a smartphone?' Dad asked Mum. Dad had had the same phone for the past eight years and had only just mastered texting.

'I just want to send photos to my friends overseas,' Mum said.

'You're being naive,' Dad said. He told us we should delete all our internet accounts, but that before we deleted them we should change our names and dates of birth and locations. We should upload photos of random people and befriend strangers from the far reaches of the world. We should try to break these websites' algorithms so they couldn't work out who or what or where we were. 'These websites, they have no way of making money otherwise. They'll sell you to the highest bidder.'

'Everyone has a smartphone these days,' I said.

'If you spend more time in the real world and less time online, it might make you happier,' Dad said.

I got a friend request from Mum on Facebook a few days later. Her profile picture was one of me and her and Toby where none of us looked good. The only other thing on her profile was a video she had recorded on her smartphone. It was thirty seconds long. The first ten seconds were of her facing the camera saying that she would appreciate no one telling Dad about this, and the final twenty seconds were of her trying to work out how to stop recording.

Mum maxed out at about fifteen friends. They included me, Toby, a couple of people I recognised from her work, a woman in a floral dress, a woman with big horn-rimmed glasses, a middle-aged man in a military uniform, three people whose profile pictures were cartoons, one whose was a flower, her friend Pam who lives in Canada, and a very sexy lady.

'You know that one is just a scam,' I said.

'I thought it was Pam's daughter,' she said.

'Why would Pam's daughter want to add you?'

'I haven't seen her for five or six years,' Mum said. 'And she was always very outgoing. But I've realised it probably isn't her because she's sent me a message asking if I want to have sex.'

I told her how to delete a friend.

Mum left Dad just over a year ago. She posted a video titled 'Moving Home'. In the video she was sitting in her car. She said she had spent a long time considering it and had decided to quit her job and move back to her hometown. She was going to move in with her sister while she looked for her own place and was looking forward to starting the next phase of her life. She didn't mention Dad once. I liked the video.

Mum picked me up from the airport and dropped me off at her house before she had to go back to work. I'd seen a video of her new house that she'd posted when she first moved in. It was a three-bedroom villa on a quiet street. It had a small yard and a little space for a garden down the side. The fence was a trellis painted lilac which made the house look like it was owned by the type of person who collects crystals.

'Is there anything you want me to do while you're at work?' I asked her.

'There are a couple of pieces of furniture I haven't gotten around to putting together,' she said. 'You could do that.'

The master bedroom had her bed and drawers in it, and the lounge had a couch and the second TV she had bought a few years earlier, but the rest of the house was empty. There were a couple of big cardboard boxes in one of the rooms. There was a picture of a desk on one of them and a bookshelf on the others. I got started on the desk. The instructions said it would take two people fifteen minutes to set up. I did it alone and it took me an hour and a half. I moved Mum's computer from the kitchen table to the desk, and brought a chair from the kitchen for her to sit on.

Staying at Mum's seemed like a good opportunity to get some writing done. I set up my laptop on the kitchen table and opened a new document. I started writing a story about a middle-aged couple having a fight. The fight was about what they were going to have for dinner, but it was actually a metaphor for something deeper than that. I hadn't worked out what yet. I googled 'sources of conflict in relationships', then I ended up spending the afternoon refreshing my email inbox and on thesaurus.com clicking on all the synonyms for 'argue' (dispute, quarrel, quibble, squabble, altercate, bandy, battle).

Mum had ordered a bed for me, but it hadn't arrived yet, so I had a nap on the couch, then woke up and watched the news. For dinner I made scrambled eggs on toast. Mum came home at 10pm. She told me about how her choir had been reworking pop songs from the eighties, and they'd all gone out for dinner together afterwards. She asked how my day had been and I said I'd built the desk.

'Thanks for that,' she said. We went into the study and looked at the desk. 'Looks just like it did on the box,' she said. There were still some shelves sitting in a box, ready to be assembled.

'I can put together the shelves tomorrow,' I said.

'One thing I've been thinking you can do is paint the fence. I got a quote from some local painters, but if you wanted to do it instead, I'll give you the money.'

'I can do that.'

'I'll give you a quarter of the money now, and three-quarters when you finish.'

'You don't have to pay me,' I said. 'That's why I'm here.'

I slept on the couch. Quarter of the money arrived in my bank account the next morning.

Mum had already left by the time I woke up. I watched TV for a couple of hours. Mum only had the free channels, so I watched talk shows and infomercials. My bed arrived shortly after midday. It was a single bed with slats and a frame. I assembled it. The instructions said it would take two people half an hour to assemble. It took me two hours by myself. I found a set of brand new sheets in the hot-water cupboard. I put them on the bed and had a nap.

Mum came home at 5:30pm. She told me she usually did a cake-decorating class on Tuesdays but she was skipping it this week. She made macaroni and cheese for dinner and said she was going to have to get used to making vegetarian food. I said I would be fine with making my own dinner. Mum said she'd talked to the neighbour, who had agreed the fence was ugly, and he was happy for me to come onto his property to paint his side. I got the buckets of paint out of the boot of Mum's car.

Mum took a video of me standing in front of the fence holding two buckets of paint. 'Here's the local painter,' she said, 'also known as my son.' I lifted up one of the buckets of paint and waved at the camera. The bucket wobbled. Mum pointed her phone at the front fence and then turned it to show the other part of the fence, which went down the side of the property between her driveway and the neighbour's. 'He has a lot of work to do.'

I put the paint in the shed and we went back inside and sat at the kitchen table. Mum looked at her phone and said, 'Hmmm. What happened to your Facebook?'

'I deactivated it,' I said. 'I needed some space.'

'How will we talk then?'

'We can talk,' I said. 'We have other ways to talk.'

I heard Mum singing and banging around in the study early in the morning. I listened to ambient music on my headphones and fell back asleep. It was midday when I woke up again. I had a shower, made a plunger of coffee and some scrambled eggs, and read the newspaper for an hour before I decided to get started on the fence. I had thrown away all my old worn-out clothes when I left my flat, so I had to decide which of my nice clothes I wanted to ruin. I chose the older of my two pairs of black jeans and a T-shirt of a local band I used to be friends with. I swirled the paint with a stick, like I had seen Dad do, then poured a bit into a paint tray. I covered the paintbrush with paint and spread it on the fence. The trellis was tricky. I had to paint the front of each slat, the edges, and all the bits in between. The paint wouldn't get into all the joins and corners unless I jammed the brush right in. It took a long time and the end of the paintbrush was getting frayed. If I covered the brush very thickly with paint, the joins and corners got filled much more easily. I was a quarter of the way down the fence before I got to the end of my first tray of paint. I opened up the bucket again and stirred it with the stick. My sunscreen ran off my forehead and stung my eyes. I wiped it off with my arm and got paint all over my face, so I decided to pack it in for the day.

I had another shower and went for a walk into town. I hadn't left the property or talked to anyone who wasn't Mum in days, so I took my laptop to a café to work on my writing. I looked at the chalkboard menu and chose the cheapest item, a bowl of chips.

'Anything else?' the girl at the counter asked.

'No, not at the moment,' I said.

'I like your T-shirt,' she said.

I looked at my T-shirt. It had a cartoon cat on it. 'Thanks, I got it from an op shop.'

'Oh nice,' she said. 'That will be $5.50.'

I gave her my bank card. 'How's your day going?'

'Good, not too busy, which is nice.'

'I bet,' I said. 'Does it get boring?'

'Sometimes,' she said, 'but mostly I'm grateful.'

I entered my PIN. I saw that her T-shirt also had a cat on it. I thought about saying I liked her T-shirt too, but it was probably too late. I kept standing at the counter.

'Your number's just there,' she said and gestured to a number on a stick in front of me.

'Thanks,' I said, and took the number. I found a table near a woman who also looked like she was working. I opened my laptop and reread what I had written the day before.

Soon after I sat down, the girl came over to me and handed

me a little piece of paper with a handwritten series of numbers on it. For a moment I thought she'd given me her number but then I realised it was the Wi-Fi password. I hadn't planned to go on the internet but I entered the password anyway. She came back with my chips and I wrote another five hundred words of the argument between the couple. It was going around in circles and I couldn't figure out how to end it. Making them break up would be too obvious, so I went on the internet.

I opened Facebook without thinking and then closed the tab. I opened a new tab and couldn't think of a single other website, so I went back to Facebook and reactivated my profile. I deleted my flatmates, everyone I owed money to, everyone who had messaged me in the past couple of months, everyone I worked with, and all of the people who were close friends with all of the people I had deleted. I deleted all my photos and unliked all my hobbies. I changed my name to Frank Grimes, my profile photo to a solar eclipse and my cover photo to a house on fire. I changed my birthplace to Kitten, Sweden and my location to Hell, Michigan. I sent friend requests to random people I found all over the world. I didn't delete any of my family. I looked at my Mum's profile. Her profile picture was still the same bad photo of me and her and Toby. She had posted a video earlier that morning called 'My Wonderful Son'. I made sure my headphones were in and watched it. It was filmed in the study. The camera was pointed at the desk I had put together, and Mum said, 'My wonderful son has come to stay with me for a while, and look what he has done with my studio.' The camera panned to the shelves, which Mum must have put together. 'It's great to have a handyman around the house.' She turned the camera around so it was pointing at her face and sang, 'Why do birds suddenly appear, every time, you are near.' I liked the video and closed the tab before it ended.

The girl with the cat T-shirt sat down at a table across from me. She had a muffin and a coffee and was reading a book I recognised. Lots of people had been reading it over summer and posting about it online. They said that it was life-changing and that everyone had to read it and that it spoke to our generation in a way no other writer had ever done before. I'd told people it was on my to-read list. I looked it up on the local library website and saw that it was currently on loan, but there was a button saying 'Reserve Book' next to it. I clicked the button and it asked me to enter my membership details. I clicked on the map at the bottom of the website and saw that the library was a couple of blocks away so I packed up my things and walked there.

I couldn't complete my membership registration without proof of address. I said I didn't really have an address but I was staying with my mum for a while. They said that would do; they could send me a letter that I could bring back in to complete my registration. I asked if I could reserve a book now, and they said probably not.

At home, I unpacked some boxes of kitchen things that had been sitting in the corner, and made an omelette for dinner. Mum was at choir practice again and wouldn't get home until nine. I was watching a movie on TV when she came home. She went to bed.

I looked at the fence. All the paint I had put on the day before had dripped down, leaving teardrops all over the fence. I touched the teardrops and they were firm. I forced my fingernail under one and peeled it off. The lilac paint was underneath.

'You put it on too thick,' a man said on the other side of the fence. 'I had a look last night.' I looked through the trellis at him. He was bald and was wearing shorts high around his hips. He had long thin legs with very round knees that stuck out. There were patches of grey stubble at the tops of his cheeks that he had missed while shaving.

'What can I do about it?' I asked.

'Not much you can do now,' he said. 'You're going to have to sand it down and start again.'

'I'll have to find some sandpaper,' I said.

'I have some you can use,' he said. He disappeared into his house and came back with a piece of sandpaper smaller than the palm of my hand. He passed it through a hole in the fence.

'Thanks,' I said. I crouched down and got started near the bottom of the fence.

'You're moving your arm too much,' the neighbour said. 'Use your wrist more.' He came around the fence and stood behind me. 'Do circular motions.'

I tried to do circular motions, but the slats were too close together and I kept hitting my knuckles on the wood.

'That's more like it,' he said. He paced around behind me for a while and then leaned against the letterbox. I switched from crouching to sitting on the concrete, but it wasn't much more comfortable.

'You'll get this done in no time,' the neighbour said.

I made a noncommittal sound.

It took me about an hour to clear off half the paint from the day before. The neighbour helped himself to a series of plums from Mum's tree and talked about how the council was getting rid of the car parks on the street. I wanted to finish the sanding but my arm was tired and my legs were tired and my bum hurt and the sun had burned through the clouds and was now starting to burn my face.

'I've got an appointment,' I said to the neighbour. 'I'll do the rest tomorrow.'

I went for a walk up the river. The only other people walking were old people with dogs. None of the dogs were on leads. They would run up the trail away from their owners, pause to look back and then run back to them. Whenever two dogs met they ran around each other in circles. They were so happy to see each other. I walked past a series of swimming holes, each with groups of teenagers swimming around splashing each other, throwing balls and laughing. I walked past the first three holes before finding a fourth hole, which was deeper than the others and empty. I stripped down to my underwear and waded in. I got up to my waist and then dived under. When I resurfaced I realised I couldn't touch the bottom anymore, and I remembered a news story about a dead man they'd found up north the other day who went swimming in a river alone. I doggy-paddled back to the shallows and then sat on a rock. I could feel the current moving around my legs. A man and a woman came down the bank across the other side of the swimming hole. They looked like they were in their early forties, older than any of my friends at home, but younger than anyone else I'd come across on the path. There was no path on their side so they must have come from a private property. They dropped their towels on a grassy spot near the hole and I waved at them.

'How's the water?' the man asked. He was taking off his shirt. His chest hair had big grey patches even though his head hair was dark.

'It's nice,' I said. 'Refreshing.'

He dived into the deep end.

'I just moved here,' I said when he popped up again. 'I don't know anybody yet.'

'How are you finding it?' he said.

'It's good,' I said. 'Did you hear about the man who died while swimming up north?' I asked. 'They think he hit his head diving in.'

The woman sat at the edge of the water and lowered herself in. She kicked off from the bank and swam towards us. The man swam back and met her halfway.

I moved from the shallows to the part of the hole where it was just deep enough for me to touch the bottom on my tiptoes. I did very short laps of two or three strokes each way for a couple of minutes and then looked back at them. They had their legs and arms wrapped around each other. I tried to do a handstand in the water but could only get one hand on the ground. They were kissing. I got out of the water. My wet underwear soaked through my shorts and my wet feet got sand on them before I put them in my socks. The walk back home was very uncomfortable.

I read the newspaper and made fried eggs for dinner. I rewrote my story so that the couple were arguing over how best to deal with their son's depression as well as what to have for dinner. The dad thought the son should sort it out himself and that they should have mashed potatoes. The mum wanted baked potatoes.

I checked Facebook and Mum had just posted another video. It was titled 'My First Win'. The camera faced a chess board and Mum said, 'After ten weeks at chess club, tonight I finally had my first victory.' She zoomed in on a black king which had been knocked over. The camera wobbled as she picked up a white bishop and held it close to the lens. 'This was the winning piece.' 'We Are the Champions' by Queen played in the background and cartoon fireworks exploded over a black-and-white still of her holding the bishop.

The letter arrived the next day. I took it to the library and they gave me a library card. I tried to put the book on reserve, but an error kept appearing and no one could work out why until we realised it had been returned. I issued the book and put it in my bag and went back to the café. The girl wasn't working but the man at the counter smiled at me when I walked in. I ordered a coffee and tried to ask him how his day was going but the coffee machine started hissing and he turned away from me so I took my table number and sat down with the book. I read for half an hour and then I walked home. I held the book with its cover facing outwards so anyone who walked past me could see what it was. When I got home I sanded off the last of the teardrops on the fence. It was too hot to start painting, so I figured I would start again the next day.

Mum did not have any clubs or activities planned that evening, but it was Friday so I wanted to go out. I went to an expensive bar in an old church because it had a big courtyard with lots of chairs but not many tables. I got there early and sat at a big table with lots of seats around it. I sipped a pint while holding the book up so the cover was visible. I watched over the top of my book as the courtyard began to fill up.

Some young guys sat at the table next to mine; one was a New Zealander and one had a German accent. The New Zealander spoke about a Toyota Hilux he had just bought and how it was a great truck. He spoke about how changing gears was an absolute dream, there were no little tricks he needed to get used to, it felt as easy as driving an auto. He had never before in his life owned a car he felt as in control of. It was nice for him to feel so in control. The other man nodded along. A dog showed up in the courtyard. It ran around visiting tables one by one for a pat.

'That's a cute dog,' the New Zealander said, and I decided I liked him. I waited for the dog to come to us. I wanted it to sit in between our tables so that I could shuffle my chair over and give it a great big pat, and the two men would come over and pat it as well and they would tell me about their trucks and I could tell them about the book I was reading and we would agree that it was a very cute dog. The dog's owner whistled and it ran back over to the other side of the courtyard. I finished my pint and some people took some of the chairs from around my table away to other tables so I left.

I slept late on Saturday. Mum was already gone when I woke up, so I got started on the fence. The neighbour showed up after about an hour with a deck chair and the newspaper and sat on his side of the fence watching. He yelled out crossword clues to me, then yelled out the answers before I had a chance to say anything. I wiped the brush on the side of the tray until there was barely any paint left on the brush, then wiped that against the fence. The small amount of paint left on the brush only lasted a couple of strokes before I had to put more on again. I had to go over all the connecting bits several times before the paint got into all the cracks.

After a couple of hours I stood back and looked at the fence. I had only completed about three metres, not even half of one side, and I could still see the lilac paint under the white. I would have to do a second coat the next day.

'Giving up already,' the neighbour called from his stoop when he saw me packing up the paint.

'Yep,' I said. 'Giving up is what I do best.'

I made an omelette for dinner and went for a walk. I walked through a park into some forest and around a winding path up a hill. At the top of the hill there was a lookout with a monument and an information placard. On one side you could see the town, the harbour, and across the harbour a mountain range silhouetted by the setting sun. On the other side there was a river that carved its way through a valley surrounded by rolling hills. There were half a dozen tourists at the lookout, pointing in different directions, trying to work out where they had been or where they were going to go. I took off my headphones and stood near them and watched the sun set.

'Can you help me with something?' Mum yelled out from the study when she heard me get home. 'When you have time.'

I went into the study and she was standing on a chair holding a green bedsheet.

'Good,' she said. Her teeth were clenched around three drawing pins. 'You're here.'

I took the sheet from her and held my hand out for her to spit the drawing pins into.

'I'm putting this up on the wall as a green screen,' she said.

'Will it work?' I said. 'It's just a sheet.'

'It's just a bit of fun,' she said.

I handed her the corner of the sheet and she hung it up on the wall. I managed to jump up and stick the other corner up with a drawing pin. The middle of the sheet flopped down so we stuck one in there too.

Mum spent all the next day in the study with her new green screen. I sat in the kitchen writing. I rewrote the story so that the son wasn't actually depressed; instead the couple were arguing about what they would do if their son happened to be depressed. I decided it was better if they weren't arguing about dinner at all.

At the end of the day Mum posted another video called

'Just a Bit of Fun'. In it Mum was wearing a stripy shirt and standing in front of the Eiffel Tower. You could see the fold lines from the green sheet. Accordion music played in the background.

'Bonjour,' she said. 'I'm just on a wee holiday in France. Wish you could be here with me.' She disappeared off-screen to return a few seconds later, wearing a beret and holding a baguette, before she started laughing uncontrollably. She hit the sheet with the top of the baguette and one corner fell off the wall, bringing the Eiffel Tower down with it.

In the comments she wrote, 'A friend has offered me a proper green screen so next time you see me it will be a lot more professional.'

'I've been looking at the fence,' the neighbour told me as I was setting up to start painting it again. 'I reckon it would be beneficial if you sanded the rest of it down too.'

'Okay,' I said. 'You don't think I should start painting it yet?'

'Well, you could,' he said. 'But the paint underneath is getting flaky, and it will take the new stuff off with it too.'

I looked at the fence and he was right.

'I'll get Mum to buy me some sandpaper,' I said.

'You don't need to do that,' he said. 'Use the stuff I gave you the other day and when that's done I'll get you some more.'

The piece of sandpaper was tiny and was already worn out, but I used it until the paper heated up from the friction and felt like my fingers were about to rip through it. The neighbour watched me, and just as it was becoming completely unusable he went into his house and returned with another piece that was just as small and slightly less worn out.

As I sanded, the neighbour leaned against the letterbox and talked about how the plums this year are smaller and less juicy than they used to be, even the ones at the supermarket. How you used to be able to find plums the size of your fist, and now they were all half that size. As he talked he helped himself to plum after plum from Mum's tree. I got about halfway down one side of the fence going down the driveway. My fingers had welts all over them from where they'd rubbed against the latticework.

Dad called me. He said he was checking on how I was getting along, but then he asked, 'How's everything going with your mum?'

'Good,' I said. 'She's doing a lot of things. I don't see her that much.'

'What is she up to anyway, is she doing dance classes still, or something else?'

'She's been mostly involved in a choir here,' I said. 'I think she still dances sometimes.'

'That's good she's getting involved with things up there.'

'She seems to be keeping busy,' I said.

'Are you keeping busy?'

I said that I'd been doing a lot of writing and that I was painting the fence, and he said painting a trellis was hard work and most people used a paint sprayer to do it. But that wasted a lot of paint, so a brush was best if you had time. I said I had plenty of time. I hadn't told him it was a trellis fence.

I told him I needed to get back to working on my story, and hung up. I got back to writing. The story felt like it was pretty much done. There wasn't a resolution, but there didn't have to be. I picked up the library book. I didn't want to waste the time I had with the book by reading it at home, so I watched TV until Mum came home.

'I think Dad is watching your videos,' I told her.

'Why do you think that?' Mum asked.

'He called me and was trying to get me to tell him more about your activities. It felt like he knows a lot already.'

'Oh, does he,' she said.

'I can show you how to change your privacy settings so only your friends can see them.'

'He can watch all he likes,' Mum said. 'I have nothing to hide.'

Mum's videos got flirtier after that. She started wearing bright red lipstick and she talked slowly, looking directly into the camera. She ended each video by blowing a kiss. I stopped watching them.

It took me the rest of the week to sand down both sides of the two parts of the fence. The neighbour would come out for an hour or two at a time and give me tiny pieces of used sandpaper from his collection. He told me all about working on the telephone lines, and when they had car-free days in the seventies, and how his son had moved to Melbourne and now supported the Australian rugby team.

I started walking up the hill to the lookout every evening. I carried my book with me to the top and sat reading in the last of the evening light. I read the information panel again and again until I had memorised it. I always took my earbuds out of my ears before I got to the top. 'Nice sunset,' I said every night to a new group of tourists at the top.

Mum invited her choir around for lunch. It was a woman named Carol's birthday and Mum had decorated a cake with her name made out of musical notes on it. The ladies from the choir kept asking what I was doing with my life. I answered the same thing each time. 'I'm painting the fence.'

When they started singing, I escaped and set up to paint again.

All the choir ladies came out of the house and told me I was doing a good job as they went past.

'They'll have to find a new place to park next time,' I said to Mum after she waved them goodbye.

'Why's that?'

'The council is getting rid of the parks on the street,' I said.

Mum and I looked at the part of the fence I had painted. The paint looked thin. 'I think it could use another coat,' she said.

I agreed, and packed up for the day. I went for a walk up the hill. At the top, a group of tourists were looking in the direction of the town hall. 'That's the town hall,' I said, pointing. 'And that's the Warehouse.' I pointed out the big red building near the town hall, in case they needed a landmark they knew.

'Your brush is too big,' the neighbour said a few days later. 'That's why it's taking so long. You can't get into all the cracks with a brush like that.'

He went inside and returned with a brush about a quarter of the size of my one. The paint sank into the cracks easily.

'Thanks,' I said.

'You can use that but give it back when you're done,' he said. He stood near the plum tree and talked about how the people who owned this house before Mum had a goat in the backyard, and when the council came to talk to them about the goat they hid it inside and claimed they never had a goat. But they did have a goat. He had seen the goat.

When I noticed people looking at the monument at the top of the hill I told them when it was erected and the meaning behind it. How the Lions Club raised money for it. I also told

129

them about the history of the path and that it was carved out to commemorate the turn of the twentieth century. All of this information could be found on the information placard, which I was leaning on so no one else could read it.

I rewrote the story again. The couple's son wasn't depressed, or maybe he was but they weren't sure. They weren't having dinner and they weren't even having an argument. They didn't talk about their son or about anything. They were just sitting in a room in silence thinking about how much they hated each other.

I studied maps of the area. I learned the name of every mountain and hill and how high they were and the tracks that went around them and how long it took to walk each track. I memorised the distances and the names of the huts. I would stand at the lookout and point to the mountain range and tell tourists everything I knew. I knew where the river came from before it got to the valley and where the fault lines that shaped the landscape were. I knew all the wildlife in the area and I knew which trees were native and which ones were introduced. I pointed at birds that came out at dusk and told the tourists what their names were in Māori and English. The tourists listened politely and then went back down the hill.

I had been working on the fence for a month and had only finished painting about half of it. I had turned pink even though I wore sunscreen every day, and my painting clothes smelled like chemicals, and they and my body were constantly damp. I never got around to washing my clothes because I wore them every day.

'This is taking forever,' I said to the neighbour.

'It's because you only work for an hour a day,' he said.

'I have other things to do,' I said. 'While I'm here.'

'Is it good to be home for a while?'

'This isn't my home. It's Mum's home. I'm just staying for a while.'

'Where is your home then?'

'I'm not really sure anymore,' I said.

'What's wrong with where you were before?' he asked.

'It was just the same thing over and over again,' I said.

'Sometimes you have to do the same thing over and over again,' he said. 'Like if you ever want to finish painting a fence.'

I put my paintbrush down in the tray and sat on the ground.

'What do you do at home?' he said. 'Over and over again?'

'I don't really do anything,' I said. 'Not during the weekdays. And then in the weekends I follow my friends around who know about parties happening in suburbs I have never been to before. We scull drinks in car parks or on the street so that we're drunk enough by the time we arrive. And then at two or three in the morning I end up standing on the outside of a circle in the smokers' area, watching other people have a conversation, smoking cigarettes I don't want. And every time, no matter where I am, I find myself standing under a drip. Every weekend I stand there and feel it dripping on the same part of the back of my head, running the same line through my hair and down the same part of my back.'

'Okay,' he said. He bit into a plum. 'That doesn't sound like a very good time.'

'Not really.'

'You know –' He paused for a moment and his mouth hung open. 'I don't know if this is helpful, but you know you don't have to stand under that drip.'

———

The days were getting shorter, and that night it got dark before I reached the lookout. I leaned against the monument and recited the words on the information panel out loud to myself because there was no one else up there. When I got back to Mum's, I bought a ticket for a flight back home that was leaving in two days.

I was up before Mum and was painting the fence by 6:30. By midday I had covered the rest of the fence with a first coat. I went inside and fried eggs for lunch, and by the time I came back the first coat was dry so I started on the second. The bucket of paint was getting low and I had to scrape paint off the sides. It was 10pm by the time I finished. Mum had already gone to bed. I ate the dinner she'd left for me.

I woke up early the next morning and told Mum I was leaving. She called in sick and we spent the morning together. I decided to make us pancakes, but she was out of eggs. I had already measured out the flour and baking powder, so I found a recipe online for scones with the same quantities. I stirred the mixture and Mum sat at the kitchen table.

'Thank you for all your work on the fence,' she said.

'No worries. Thanks for having me.'

'It has made this house feel much more like home,' she said.

'I think I will need that money,' I said.

'Do you need it now?'

'Yeah. I will need it to get a new flat.'

'Okay,' she said. 'I can find some money for you.' We took the scones out of the oven and ate them hot with cream and jam. The cream melted on the scones and left puddles on my plate, which I mopped up with more scones. She took out her phone. I asked if she was going to make another video and she said she didn't have to. She put her phone away.

'What happened to your proper green screen?' I asked her.

'Well, it was blue so it wouldn't have worked.'

'I think it can work with any colour.'

'But my eyes are blue,' she said. 'It wouldn't work.' I didn't look in her eyes, but I knew from the sound of her voice that they were filling with tears.

I knocked on the neighbour's door and he opened it slightly and looked at me over a security chain, then he unlatched it and opened the door. He was wearing a dressing gown and I noticed how much loose skin he had around his neck. The hallway behind him was stacked to the ceiling with plastic crates and newspapers.

'I just wanted to tell you I am leaving,' I said.

'Where are you going?'

'Back home,' I said.

'When are you off?' he asked.

'In about an hour.'

'I had a look at the fence this morning,' he said. 'It looks good.'

'Thanks,' I said. I looked past him. The curtains at the back of his hallway were closed. 'I've got your paintbrush,' I said. I held it out to him. I noticed a long vein that went all the way from his wrist to his elbow. 'Also, can you do me a favour? Could you return a library book for me?'

'I s'pose I can,' he said. 'Was it a good book?'

'I didn't finish it,' I said and handed it to the neighbour.

I stayed on Toby's couch for a week and put together a CV. All it said was that I knew how to make coffee and had a degree. I said I was a hard worker and was willing to work early mornings, nights, and weekends. I didn't put any references down.

When I got home from handing my CV out to every café in town, Toby said I should watch the video Mum had just posted that day. It was titled 'My Last Video'. I thought it must be about me leaving. It seemed very dramatic. Her eyes were red but her voice was strong. 'I need to tell you all something,' she started. There had been a man. He had added her and said he'd gone to school in New Zealand for a year with someone with her name. He said he had been looking for her for years, but had only found her once she'd changed her name back to her maiden name. Mum couldn't quite remember him, but she kept messaging him anyway. She liked talking to him. He wanted to move back to New Zealand to be with her, but all his money was tied up in a house in America. There was a pool that needed repairs, and he needed to get the lawn professionally re-sown. After Mum sent him some money to fix those things up, he sent her photos of the house that the real-estate agent had taken, but then he needed more money to pay for advertising. It was a nice house and it needed to attract the right market. 'It did cross my mind he wasn't who he said he was,' she said. 'But he wasn't even that handsome.' She said not to be worried, and she wasn't going to do anything stupid, but she wasn't going to post videos anymore. I liked the video.

3

ON THE EDGE OF TOWN

Mum pulls the car over on the edge of town. 'I just want to say a quick goodbye to Toby,' she says. Granddad, Aunty Ingrid and I get out of the car and follow her into the bed store.

Mum looks around and spots Toby at the back. He's wearing a yellow and black polo shirt with a name tag on it. Mum walks towards him, stopping every now and then to glance at a bed as if she is browsing.

I find the most expensive bed in the store. It's a California King, as wide as it is long, with a memory foam mattress and a motorised adjustable base with a remote control to elevate the head or feet. I sit on the California King and watch Toby talking to a man and a woman. The man is dressed in an open-collared shirt and jeans, like a rich person trying to be casual. The young woman looks bored; she's tying her hair into a ponytail. Aunty Ingrid comes over and sits next to me.

'What do you reckon,' I say to Aunty Ingrid. 'Couple, or father and daughter?'

'Don't be disgusting,' she says.

'But what do you think?'

'She must be his daughter.'

'I dunno,' I say. 'I hope so.'

We watch Mum move towards Toby, rustling through her handbag. Granddad joins us on the bed. We shuffle over. It easily fits the three of us. He's holding two cups of water and gives one to Aunty Ingrid.

'What do you think, Granddad?' I ask. 'Couple, or father and daughter?'

He looks at them and says, 'Could be either really, couldn't it?'

Mum stands on her tiptoes, trying to make eye contact with Toby from behind the couple. She's holding a scrunched-up ball of red napkins and waving it at him.

The middle-aged man grabs the young woman's hand. 'Bingo,' I say.

Aunty Ingrid drinks her entire cup of water in one go. 'That's just wrong,' she says, and crushes her plastic cup.

Toby and the couple walk down our aisle towards the front of the store. Mum follows. Aunty Ingrid and I turn our heads and watch the couple leave. Granddad stays facing the back of the store and takes a sip from his cup of water.

Toby does a 180, walks straight past Mum and comes to us. 'Hey guys, what are you doing here?' he says.

Mum follows, holding the red napkins up to him in cupped hands. 'Just wanted to give you these,' she says. The napkins unfurl to reveal three bliss balls.

'Thanks Mum,' he says. 'I've just had my break, so I'll have to wait until the end of my shift to eat them.'

'That's okay,' she says. 'It's just a token gesture.'

'If you put them in the kitchen I'll have them later. Thanks for stopping by.'

Aunty Ingrid, Granddad and I stand up. 'Well, it was nice to see you, boy,' Granddad says and shakes Toby's hand. We head towards the door and Toby walks with us, stopping to greet another couple as they walk in the doors. They're young, around thirty, in nice clothes, like they've dressed up especially.

'You all right there?' Toby says. He makes a slight hand gesture to us that simultaneously says 'Bye', 'Thanks' and 'I have to get back to work'. Mum crumples the napkins around the bliss balls.

'We're just browsing,' the couple says.

'All right,' Toby says. 'Let me know if you need any help.'

As the doors open automatically in front of us, Mum calls out, 'Hold on a minute.' We turn and see she has stopped several metres behind us. She is gripping the bliss balls tight in her fist. She has probably squished them into one big bliss ball. 'This is the last chance I have to see my son this year,' she says, as if the year isn't ending in less than a week.

Toby approaches the couple and says, 'I'll just show you a couple of really good deals we've got going in the back,' and leads them away.

Mum sits on the closest bed and watches them disappear to the back of the store. Aunty Ingrid sits next to her. 'He's working,' she says

Mum shoves the big bliss ball into her mouth. 'Then we'll wait,' she says, chewing.

Granddad looks at his watch. 'We've still got a bit of time,' he says. 'No one's got work in the morning.'

'You've been thinking of getting a new bed, haven't you, Dad?' Mum asks. 'No harm in having a bit of a look around.'

I feel light-headed. 'I'm going to get some air,' I say. I walk to the door, which opens automatically and lets in a burst of cold air. Outside, cars pass by in an unbroken line. It's early afternoon but the sky is dark grey; it has been every day since Christmas Eve, and half the cars have their lights on. The bed store is surrounded, on both sides and across the road, by identical concrete block warehouses that are all closed for the holidays. They're painted bright primary colours, darkened at the bottom from car exhaust. I drag my finger along the side of one of the warehouses and pick up black dust. I wipe the dust on my jacket. Behind the warehouses across the road there are hills covered in bush. I can't see any gaps in the warehouses leading to the bush, not that I could cross the road even if I wanted to. The footpath is muddy, and I'm not sure where the mud came from. The sky is spitting and making small dark marks on my jacket. I hold my hand out and feel the rain hit my skin like tiny needles and I'm unsure if the feeling is painful or not. I walk five minutes down the road, looking for people outside of cars, or for other shops, but there are only concrete walls and corrugated garage doors, so I turn around and walk back to the bed store.

Mum, Granddad and Aunty Ingrid are lying in three Queens next to one another. Their luggage from the car is scattered across the floor between Aunty Ingrid's and Granddad's beds. Granddad has his cap over his eyes and is snoring. There's a new cup of water on the bedside table between him and my aunty. On the table between Mum and Aunty Ingrid there is a cup stuffed with red napkins.

I sit on the bed across the aisle from my mum, who's flicking through a bed catalogue. 'You brought the bags in,' I say to Mum.

'Couldn't just leave them in the car. They'd get nicked,' Granddad says from under his hat, and then he starts snoring again.

'Look at your granddad,' Mum says. 'He'll sleep anywhere.' She laughs.

'Seems like a pretty good place to sleep to me,' I say, and

flop back on the bed with my feet on the floor. I close my eyes and try to remember how to meditate. I breathe in through my mouth and out through my nose. I can't remember the number I'm meant to count to between breaths, or if I'm meant to count at all. I have to keep pushing myself up with my feet to stop myself sliding off the bed. Somewhere in the background, behind Granddad's snores, I can hear a radio playing easy-listening music. It's playing quietly and I can't quite make out the melody or lyrics. I try to forget my breathing and focus on the music but I'm interrupted.

'If you're going to lie on the bed, lie on it properly,' someone says.

I open my eyes and see a moustached man standing over me. He's wearing the same yellow and black polo shirt as Toby, except his has the name Gerard stitched onto the front.

'My shoes are dirty,' I say, and hold a foot up towards him. The sole is wet and muddy from the footpath outside.

'That's what these are for,' he says, and pats the plastic at the foot of the bed. I hadn't noticed it before. I sit up and look around and all the other beds have the same plastic on them. I scoot up to the top of the bed and put my feet on the plastic.

'I'm not buying a bed,' I say.

'Of course you're not. Your jacket is held together with tape,' he says, pointing at the duct tape I used to patch up a rip on my sleeve months earlier. 'Don't worry about it, but if any real customers come looking, make yourself scarce.'

Gerard leaves, and Aunty Ingrid says, 'Where did you get your bed from when you moved into your flat?'

'Salvation Army,' I say.

'You didn't! What if someone died in it?' she says.

'I guess it happens.'

'You know, Toby can get you a discount here,' Mum says.

I look at the sign under the plastic under my feet. '$1999 SLEEPEZY FINANCE AVAILABLE'. 'My bed's fine,' I say.

'You better be using a mattress protector,' Mum says. 'You never know what's in old beds.'

'What's a mattress protector?' I ask.

'It's a padded layer to put between your sheet and the mattress,' Mum says.

'Oh yeah. I have one of those,' I say, 'but it also came from the Salvation Army.'

Mum shakes her head. 'Oh, to be young again,' she says.

I lie back down and try to focus on the radio but I can't. Mum and Aunty Ingrid are talking about mattress protectors.

'I've got a memory foam mattress protector,' Aunty Ingrid says. 'It's great.'

'But that's not real memory foam,' Mum says. 'You've got to get the official memory foam. Toby got me a real official memory foam pillow for Christmas.'

'Mine's real memory foam,' Aunty Ingrid says. 'It better be, the amount I paid for it.'

'Where did you get it from,' Mum says. 'You need to get the real stuff from an authorised retailer.'

'I think I got it on the internet,' Aunty Ingrid says. 'Or maybe it was from the TV.'

'This is real memory foam,' Mum says. 'See how when you press it down it stays? It's good for your back. This place is one of the only authorised retailers in town.' I open my eyes and look at Mum. She's holding a slice of pizza and more red napkins. 'If I was going to buy a new mattress, it would definitely be memory foam.' She bites into the pizza.

I roll across the bed and fall to the floor. My head misses the bedside table.

'You okay there?' Mum asks.

'I don't like beds anymore,' I say.

'Have you tried this memory foam one? It's from an authorised retailer,' Aunty Ingrid says. She and Mum laugh.

'I hate memory foam,' I say, and slap the bed. My handprint leaves a slight indent on the bed. It's official memory foam.

'Dad,' Mum yells. 'Dad!' She thumps the bedside table next to her. Her napkin-filled cup falls to the floor. He snorts and sits up. 'You're looking for a new bed, aren't you? Have you thought about memory foam?'

'What the hell is memory foam,' he says.

I lean against the bed and open the drawer in the bedside table. There's a laminated piece of A4 paper in it. It's yellow with red block letters that say 'FREE WITH SLEEPEZY FINANCE!' I open the second drawer and there's another piece of paper that says 'NOT ENOUGH SPACE. UPGRADE FOR JUST $49!'

'What a deal,' I say.

I hold on to the side of the bed and pull myself up to my feet. I check the bedside table on the other side of the bed and it has identical signs in the drawers. I walk to the back of the store and check the larger bedside tables. Their signs say 'JUST $49 WITH SLEEPEZY FINANCE' in both drawers. On one of the signs there is a penis drawn in Vivid. I pick the sheet up out of the drawer to show to my family, but as I arrive I realise I don't want to do that, so I fold it up and put it in my back pocket.

'I'm just saying it's worth having a look,' Mum says.

'It'd cost an arm and a leg getting it back home,' Granddad says.

'Yeah, but you can't get these ones back home. They don't have proper memory foam ones there.'

'I've never had a memory foam mattress before,' he says.

'Why would I need one now?'

'Well, let's ask Toby,' she says. 'He gets a staff discount.'

I go back to the California King. I lie on it and use the remote to raise its head up so I can see my family lying in their Queens. I lower the head back down and look up at the ceiling. I raise the foot of the bed up and look at the plastic sheet and its upside-down price under my feet. I raise the head up and lay on the bed contorted in a V shape, and close my eyes. I wonder if anyone sleeps like this.

'Gerard told me to tell you to stop doing that,' Toby says. I lower my feet and see him standing at the end of the bed. He points to the moustached man watching me. I roll off the bed and fall to the floor. I look up at Toby and notice that the name tag on his shirt says 'Tobias'.

'Your name isn't Tobias,' I say.

'Someone who used to work here was called Tobias,' Toby said. 'They thought it was close enough.'

'Do they call you Tobias?'

'Can you just put the bed back to normal,' Toby says.

'Sorry,' I say. I grab the remote control from the side of the bed and make the bed flat again.

'No worries,' he says. 'People do it every day.' He picks up the pillows and fluffs them.

I get up off the floor and feel plastic poke the back of my leg. 'Someone drew a penis on one of your signs,' I say, and hand him the laminated paper. It now has big white fold marks in it.

'Oh yeah, that was me the other day,' he says. 'Finally someone noticed.' He unfolds the sign and looks at it and laughs. 'You can keep it if you want,' he says, and hands it back to me.

'Gee, thanks.' I look at the penis. It's got a big vein running down the shaft. 'I'll keep this forever.' I fold the sign back up and put it back in my pocket. 'I think Mum wants to talk to you about memory foam.'

We walk back to our family, who are standing at the end of the store in front of a King.

'It's ten thousand, but it's real memory foam,' Mum says to Granddad.

'I've only got four or five years in me. I'm not spending ten thousand on a bed,' he says.

'Don't say that, Dad,' Mum says. 'You could live to a hundred.'

'I have no interest in living to a hundred.'

'Plus it's adjustable, it'll help you get out of bed in the morning.'

'I can get out of bed just fine,' he says.

'You might not be able to in ten years' time though.'

Toby stands between them. 'It's probably not worth the shipping,' he says.

'But then you wouldn't get any commission,' she says.

'I'm doing fine,' he says.

'What about with your staff discount,' she says.

'It'd be more hassle than it's worth,' he says. 'You can get something similar closer to home.'

'Okay,' Mum says. She pulls a red napkin bundle from her bag. 'I've brought you some cake from the party. It's lemon, your favourite.'

'Mum, I can't take it now. I'll have it later – I need to get back to work.'

'Okay, then. Let's talk business,' she says. 'How much will the shipping cost? Give me a figure.'

'Mum,' Toby says, 'you're being silly.' He turns around and walks away. There are no customers in the store so he walks towards Gerard who is standing watching us from the other side of the store.

'I don't want this bed anyway,' Granddad says. 'I don't think it'd fit.'

'If you're so concerned about money, Dad,' Mum says, 'you might as well buy a single bed since you're all alone anyway.' She sits on another bed, throws the napkins to the side, and bites into the cake.

Granddad gets on the bed and with the remote he raises the head up slightly and smiles. He tips his cap over his eyes and then lowers the head back down.

'I was just trying to help,' Mum says as she chews.

I pick up the napkins and walk back to the three Queens. I stack the luggage into a pile between the beds, pick up the cups off the floor, put the napkins in one and stack them. I walk over to the bin next to the water cooler and throw them into it. I take the penis sign out of my pocket and throw it into the bin too. Next to the bin there's a grubby lime-green couch under a laminated sign saying 'NOT FOR SALE'. It's coffee-stained and the only couch in the store. Nearby there's a door marked 'Staff Only'. I can hear the whirr of a fridge and the easy-listening music coming from a radio behind the door. I sit on the couch. It's lumpy and smells stale. I curl my legs up. My dirty shoes leave a mark on the armrest. I lay my head on the other armrest. My neck strains from the angle. I can feel the wood underneath the foam. I close my eyes and listen to the music, breathe in through my nose, count slowly to five and breathe out again.

THREE PIZZAS

I ordered three pizzas, two garlic breads and a big bottle of Pepsi. All that for just $29.99 delivered. How could I not? It is cold and I am already home.

My house is up two hundred steps from the closest road. I walk up and down these steps every day and organise my life so I don't have to walk them more than once a day. Whenever I leave the house I pack my bag full of everything I could possibly need. I take two books in case I finish the first. I take my water bottle. I take a jersey on hot days, sunscreen in winter, extra medication, my laptop and its charger, a banana. The bottom of my bag is full of compressed paper: receipts, rubbish, flyers and notes, letters taken from the mailbox halfway down the hill, vouchers for special pizza deals. My bag is heavy.

My flatmates will be home soon and they will be so grateful. They will appreciate how thoughtful and generous I am. I ordered one Margherita for me because I'm vegetarian; one Vegorama with no cheese for David, who is vegan; and one BBQ Meatlovers, mostly for Callum because he likes barbecue sauce. Plus two garlic breads and a big bottle of Pepsi that we can all share.

As well as living at the top of a hill, I work at the top of a different hill. I have to walk uphill both ways. Of course there is also the downhill at the beginning of each journey, but I rarely appreciate that. If I wanted I could bus to work, but it involves a transfer, costs nearly an hour's wages to get there and back, and takes the same amount of time as walking. Sometimes, if I'm lucky, when I'm walking home I'll zone out and not realise I'm walking uphill until I pass my letterbox. I never zone out on the way to work.

The delivery man puffs as he gives me the three pizzas, two garlic breads and big bottle of Pepsi. 'Beautiful view you've got here,' he says.

'You get used to it,' I say, thinking he is talking about the steps, until I realise he isn't.

I put the pizza in the kitchen and the big bottle of Pepsi in the fridge. I eat a couple of pieces of garlic bread. My flatmates will be home soon.

At work a woman ordered a large decaf trim mocha. A couple of minutes after ordering it she returned with the empty cup and asked, 'Is this really a large?'

'That is our large, but we can make you a coffee in a bowl if you want coffee in a bowl,' I said.

'When most people say large, they mean bowl,' the woman said. She huffed and said, 'Really?' when I charged her for a second large decaf trim mocha, which I served in a bowl that we usually serve soup in.

I recently had a drink with my old friend Rosie when she was back in town. We went to uni together and after uni was finished she went to America on a temporary visa and has stayed there, living in an urban artist commune in the Bay Area.

'You need to get out of this city,' she told me. 'You're better than this. You're an artist.'

'I'm barely even a writer,' I tell her. 'Plus I'm poor as shit, and I can't risk quitting my job for only a small chance of success.' I guess I should try to get a proper job, save some money and then move, but I don't want to make that compromise at the moment.

When twenty minutes have passed and neither of my flatmates have come home, I decide that I should have a slice or two before the pizza goes completely cold. I pour myself a big glass of Pepsi and put a few pieces of garlic bread, three pieces of Margherita and a piece of Vegorama with no cheese on a plate and take it to the lounge. I put on an episode of a TV show and eat. The Vegorama with no cheese is for David, but he can't complain some is gone, because he will still be given most of a pizza. He will still be grateful.

If I walk home at the right time I can watch the sun set twice. I walk home through the city, and if I look to the west I can see the sun descend over the hill, reflecting off windows, casting long shadows and bright orange light over everyone leaving their workplaces. Then, if I walk up my hill fast enough, the sun comes back up from behind the hill, and I can stop on the porch and watch it set again.

Rosie's art commune all live in a big warehouse together with no private spaces. They all work together in one big area and sleep together in another big area.

'We need people who can write,' she said. 'We can do the performances and make the things, but we need a good writer.'

'You haven't seen anything I've written since we were at uni,' I say.

'Yeah, but I know you have what it takes,' she says. 'You've got the right vibe. Come and stay sometime. It's fun.'

By the end of the episode of the TV show, I have gone back to the kitchen and taken another two slices of Margherita, another two slices of Vegorama with no cheese, and a slice of Meatlovers even though I am a vegetarian, because I also like barbecue sauce. I have also eaten the remaining few pieces of the first garlic bread and drunk another glass and a half of Pepsi. My flatmates still haven't returned home and the pizza has gone cold.

At work, the woman returned fifteen minutes later with the empty bowl and smacked her lips. 'That's more like it,' she said. 'I'll have another one of those.'

I made her another decaf trim mocha in a bowl that we normally serve soup in. She didn't complain about paying for this one. I don't know exactly how big the bowl was, but she must have been close to drinking a litre of milk within half an hour.

I'd always assumed that I'd be famous by now and wouldn't have to deal with this kind of thing anymore.

Rosie's urban art commune is working on a series of artworks devoted to the clitoris. It sounds like they mostly just have sex.

'I have a girlfriend,' I say. She looks at me like she is confused as to why I felt like I had to say that. 'And it doesn't really sound like my kind of thing. I need my own space.'

I take the remaining pizza, garlic bread and the half-empty bottle of Pepsi to the lounge and put them on the coffee table. When my flatmates come home soon, the pizza will be right there waiting for them. I eat a few more pieces of the Meatlovers, even though I am a vegetarian, so that there is an equal amount of pizza for Callum and David. I put on another episode of the TV show, and sit on the seat that is the farthest away from the coffee table so that I won't eat any more pizza. At the end of the episode I reach for another piece of garlic bread and find the packet empty.

A man once made me remake his coffee three times. The first time he was probably right, I'd just thrown it together without much care. When I gave it to him, he looked at me and I knew he was going to return it. The second time, I made sure to evenly tamp and wait for the pour to turn light brown and start twisting. He stuck his head over the counter and watched me watch the pour and nodded. But once he took a sip he decided it wasn't good enough again and insisted that I change the grind. When I got it right he told me, 'You should be happy, because you learned something today.'

I asked Rosie if she was seeing anyone else when she was in town. She told me that before she decided to leave, someone sent her a screenshot from a group chat with all our guy friends where they talked about how big her tits were and which one of them would get to fuck her first. I had no idea it had happened and why no one had invited me to the chat.

It's nearly midnight when I hear my flatmates coming up the steps. There are three pieces of Vegorama with no cheese, three pieces of Meatlovers, no Margherita, no garlic bread and less than a glass of Pepsi left. I stand by the door holding a pizza box in each hand.

'Surprise,' I say when they come through the door. 'I have bought you pizza.'

'Thanks,' Callum says and opens one of the boxes. 'Did you get any Margherita?'

'Please eat the pizza,' I say. 'I have eaten so much pizza.'

'Why did you get so much pizza?' David asks.

'I wanted to surprise you with pizza,' I say.

Callum and David stand by the window, watching the lights of the city as they eat. They leave the door open and the sounds of the city waft up to our house. Friday nights make sound rise. It's not just the loud sounds – cars honking, clubs pumping, people yelling – that rise up to the house; we can also hear the street cleaners sweeping the gutters and cars driving through puddles. I rub my chest and try to push the acid back down to my stomach.

'Also today someone ordered a flat white for their dog, and I thought they were joking, but then I saw the dog licking the cup and that fucked me up. It was really fucked up.'

SYNDROME

I am walking home from work. It's the type of hot where the air feels like custard. I told myself when I got this job that I would write every day after work, and if I didn't I couldn't call myself a writer. My computer is broken so I stop at the library to use the ones there.

The air inside the library is even thicker than outside, like the custard has formed a skin. I buy a Sprite from the vending machine and drink it quickly before all the bubbles can escape. I hold a burp in, and it explodes in my chest and hurts a bit. All the computers are being used so I write by hand, which is useless, because my handwriting is illegible and I'm writing trash. I pick up a book I have been intending to read for a long time and open it up on the table in front of me.

I'm dripping. I drip onto the table and make a small pool. I try to wipe it away with my arm, but it streaks and the pool divides into many small puddles. I drip onto the library book. Every drip reveals secret backwards letters. I look at a librarian and she looks back and shakes her head. I close the book and put it aside.

I go back to my notebook and write a physical description

of my ex-girlfriend in the kindest way possible. I run out of breath. It feels like there is a pillow on my face and someone is sitting on it. I put my head in my hands and scrunch my eyes closed. Sweat pools into my hands and I'm underwater. When I lift my head and move my hands, the pool falls onto my notebook and destroys my writing. I try to rewrite the description, but my pen rips through the wet paper. I scribble all over the page, ripping up the entire thing.

A library employee has a small handheld vacuum and is kneeling down and sucking up a pile of crumbs, and with it all the air in the area. People are marching into the library, gulping mouthfuls of air and leaving before they exhale. Every time they do, the air gets thicker. I am denser than I have ever been before. I check out the book and leave.

I buy a pack of cigarettes from the petrol station across the road from the library and walk home smoking. The smoke goes right inside me the way the air was not. It feels like I have finally surfaced after being underwater all day.

As soon as I'm through the door I take off my T-shirt. It's soaked through. I have to peel it off. I drop it on the floor by the door in the hallway. I take off my jeans once I get to my bedroom and lay face-down on my duvet. The duvet is warm against my skin so I push it out from under me and kick it to the floor at the foot of my bed. It's still too hot. I get up and open all the windows, then push my bed under the windows so I can drink in all the air as it comes through. The sheets are scratchy so I rip them off and throw them on a pile on top of the duvet. I also throw the pillows onto the pile and the mattress protector. I lay on the mattress, which has a cool plasticky feel, and drip.

My phone rings. I hang off the bed and reach into the pocket of my jeans. It's an unknown number.

'Hello?'

'Hi. It's Dennis here, from the computer store.'

'Hello.'

'I'm just calling to say, we've worked out what the issue is. And, unfortunately, it's going to be a bit pricier than we anticipated.'

'Okay.'

'As it's a hardware issue, we are going to have to spend some money on parts, and that will probably be twice as much as our original estimate.'

'Okay.'

'So we're just checking in that that's okay before we do the work.'

'That's okay.'

'Great, we will get onto it right away.'

'When will the computer be ready?'

'I'm sorry, I cannot understand what you're saying.'

'When. Will. I. Be. Able. To. Pick. Up. My. Computer?' I say.

'I'm sorry, I think our connection might be bad.'

'Day?'

'Are you asking when it will be ready?'

'Yes.'

'It will be ready tomorrow. Can I confirm you will pick it up then?'

'Yes. I'll see you tomorrow.'

I don't have the money, but I don't tell him that. I drop my phone next to my ear. I hear the man say goodbye, then hang up when I don't respond. I throw the phone into the pile of sheets. I let my arm fall back onto the mattress and it lands in an odd position above my head. I try to move it down to next to my body, where it should be, but I can't. I feel flat, like a painting. I try to roll over but no parts of my body are moving. I close my eyes, then realise that it was a mistake because I can't open them again. I'm not sure how long I stay in this position because time seems to stop working as normal. I hear my flatmate come home.

'Hey,' he yells out.

I try to respond but I can't.

'Hey,' he says again, closer this time.

I open my mouth and close it but no sound comes out.

'You all right?' he says. He's in my room.

I try to say no, but a different sound comes out. I feel my mattress sink as my flatmate sits down.

'What's happening?'

I make another noise.

'Can you move?'

'No.' I manage to say it this time. He grabs my hand and lifts up my arm. He lets it go and it falls back to where it was on the mattress. I open my eyes and see him holding my wet T-shirt.

'Do you need to go to the hospital?'

I make an affirmative sound.

He calls his sister because she's the only person we know with a car. They're not currently speaking but she comes around anyway.

'Can you walk?' my flatmate asks.

'I don't know.'

He puts his shoulder under my armpit and pushes his hand between my back and the mattress and lifts me up, but once I'm in his arms I realise that I can actually walk. I put on a clean T-shirt and a pair of shorts and walk slowly down the steps to the car double-parked outside.

'What's happening?' my flatmate's sister asks.

'I don't know,' I say.

We start driving to the hospital, and when we're nearly there I realise that this is all just a panic attack, and that I don't want to be part of the statistic of people who arrive at the hospital thinking they're in danger when it's just a panic attack.

'Stop,' I say, 'don't take me to the hospital.'

'What?'

'It's fine. I'm fine. Don't worry about me.'

'Well, we're here now so we might as well make sure.'

We pull into the emergency department. I don't want to get out of the car, but I do when my flatmate tries to pick me up again. He holds my arm and guides me to the entrance. His sister drives away to find a park.

'It's just a panic attack. Probably,' I say to the woman at the counter.

She looks at me and says, 'Have a seat. You can do the paperwork later.'

My flatmate and I sit on some plastic seats that are attached to other plastic seats with a metal rod, like at an airport. I watch a child push over a pile of blocks and laugh. The child's laugh is slow and deep, like an adult who is trying to tease me. I have not been sitting for long when a nurse calls my name.

I leave my flatmate and follow the nurse to a room. In the room there is a bed, an eye chart, a mirror, a computer and a chair. She hands me a pile of folded material. As I take it the pile unfolds itself into a gown. 'Change into this,' she says. 'I'll be right back.' I look into the mirror and see my hair is dark and sticking to my forehead. I look like I have been swimming in my clothes. I am very pale apart from my cheeks which are very red.

A doctor comes into the room with a clipboard, looks at me and says, 'Well, it's definitely more than a panic attack.'

She notices I'm looking at the eye chart and asks how my vision is. In the waiting room it felt like I could see absolutely everything very clearly, but now that I'm looking at the chart I can't make out any single letter, only the chart as a whole.

'I think it's okay. Maybe a bit blurry,' I say.

She asks if I'm on any medication and I tell her about my antidepressants. She asks if I took too many pills on purpose and I tell her that I didn't. She writes something down on a piece of paper attached to her clipboard.

'Are you a smoker?' she asks.

'No,' I say, then realise she can probably smell smoke on me. 'But I do smoke sometimes.'

'So you are a smoker.'

'No,' I say, 'it's just sometimes it's the only way I feel like I can breathe all the way in and out like a normal person.'

'There are plenty of other techniques that can help with your breathing.'

'I know,' I say. 'It's a coping mechanism. Sometimes it's the only thing that can calm me down.'

'But cigarettes don't calm you down,' she says. 'They do the complete opposite. When you smoke it triggers a release of adrenaline. It increases your heart rate. It increases respiration and perspiration.'

'I never said it was a good coping mechanism,' I say.

'No, it's not,' she says. She looks down at the chart and back at me. 'The nurse will be back in a few minutes.' She leaves.

I realise I am still holding the gown the nurse gave me. I take off my T-shirt and shorts and pull the gown down over my shoulders. There's a knock at the door and my flatmate and his sister enter. 'You've got it on backwards,' my flatmate's sister says. I untie the bow at the gown's front and it falls into a pile on the ground. She picks it up and holds it in front of me.

'Arms out,' she says. I put my arms out and she puts the sleeves around my arms, pushes my shoulder so I turn around, and ties it up at the back. I sit down on the chair.

The nurse returns and tells me to get onto the bed. My flatmate and his sister stand with their backs touching the wall, so they're as far out of the way as possible. She takes my temperature and heart rate and tests my blood pressure. She pulls the blankets over me but I push them off.

'Is it bad?' I ask.

'Well, it's definitely more than a panic attack.'

She finds a vein in my arm and sticks a needle into it, which she attaches to a tube that leads to a vial. Blood comes out of my arm and into the vial with no suction or pressure, as if it never wanted to be in there in the first place. The nurse switches out the vial, and then does so again, and then again. She puts four different stickers on the four different vials and puts them in a plastic container. No blood is spilled.

She detaches the tube from the needle but leaves the needle in my arm. 'We're going to put you on a drip to try and get this temperature down,' she says.

'Thank you.'

'Do you have a headache?'

'No,' I say, but as soon as I've said it I realise I do actually have a headache. 'Actually I do have a headache,' I say.

'Yes, you will be dehydrated. This should fix that.' She attaches a new tube to the needle in my arm. This one leads to a bag of clear liquid hanging next to the bed. While she does this I try to work out if I have a headache or if this is just what it feels like to have a head.

The nurse leaves and a different doctor comes in. He introduces himself but I forget his name instantly. 'I'm the resident psychologist here,' he says.

'Hi,' I say.

'And how do you feel, how do you feel?' he says.

'Like I haven't breathed in a really long time,' I say.

'And how have you been feeling lately?'

'I guess not good.'

'I know you have been asked this before, but I just have to make sure that you didn't take too many pills on purpose.'

'No, I didn't.'

'So you took too many pills accidentally.'

'I don't think I did.'

'Okay. And have you taken any substances in the past few days?'

'No.'

'Have you been more depressed than usual lately?'

'Yes. I just had a break-up.'

'Have you been having any suicidal thoughts lately?'

'Yes, but I always do.'

'And this was not self-inflicted? You're not in trouble, we just have to know.'

'It wasn't.'

'Do you think it's possible you accidentally took too many pills.'

'I guess that is possible.'

'So what it looks like is that you accidentally took your dose twice, and we are just waiting for the blood tests to confirm.'

'I really don't think that's what happened, but I guess so.'

He gives me some forms to fill out. I try to fill them out myself, but I can't remember my phone number or address. My flatmate fills out the rest of the forms for me and then I sign it. My signature is pointier than usual.

Soon after, a man in blue scrubs comes and pushes my bed out of the room and into a ward. He doesn't slow down for anyone and the people in front of us have to jump out of the way. He is very efficient. My flatmate and his sister follow behind us, carrying my clothes. When I'm in the ward a nurse comes and tells them visiting hours are over and they have to leave. The nurse pulls the curtains shut as soon as they take a step away, so I can't see them leaving. She takes my temperature again and notes it down on a clipboard. She changes the drip and tells me to go to sleep. I haven't had dinner and am hungry but I don't mention it, because sick people are not meant to care about food. During the night I wake up several times and feel the hospital air needling the inside of my face, behind my cheekbones.

In the morning I wake up and need to pee, but I am not sure how to leave my bed because I still have a tube attached to my arm. I yell out for help. A nurse comes and tells me not to yell, then shows me a call button attached to my bed. She detaches the drip and I get up and find the toilet. I was expecting my legs to be weaker than they are. I feel hazy but okay. After I go to the toilet I see a sign labelled EXIT and I think for a second about following it and going home, but I don't have any shoes with me and I'm starting to feel light-headed. I go back to my bed and the nurse reattaches my tube. She shows me that the drip bag is hanging on a pole on wheels, so next time I need to go to the toilet I can take it with me.

For breakfast I am given two pieces of white toast, some butter in a small plastic container with a tearaway foil lid, and scrambled eggs, which are in an oval-shaped patty. To drink I'm given a plastic cup of orange juice. For breakfast dessert, there is a small plastic bowl of fruit salad with an elasticated piece of plastic, like a hair net, covering it. I know it is breakfast dessert and not part of the main meal because the food comes with a piece of paper which lists all the food items under the headings 'DRINK', 'BREAKFAST' and 'DESSERT'. I'm told I am not allowed tea or coffee because they could dehydrate me further. The food is okay.

After breakfast my flatmate arrives with my phone, the library book and my water bottle. 'I thought you'd want these,' he says.

'Thanks.'

'Sorry I didn't bring you any food, I know the food here is terrible.'

'It's not terrible. It's okay.'

'You don't need to lie, I know it's terrible.' He sits in the chair next to the bed. 'You know, me and my sister are getting lunch today. After yesterday we thought it was about time we settle things.'

'Oh, cool. I guess you're welcome.'

'She's worried about you.'

'Oh, okay.'

'And she wants to know – and I guess I do too – that this was an accident.'

'Yeah. I don't know what happened but it wasn't on purpose.'

'Good. I didn't think it was. She just, she knows you sometimes get down.'

'Yeah. Well, I didn't. Not this time.' I look at my phone. I have five unread emails and no text messages. The battery is on 5 percent.

'Do you think you can bring my charger in?' I ask him.

'Yeah, totally. Can I bring it after work? I'm already running late.'

'Yeah, that's okay,' I say.

'If you need it I can go home now. I'm sure my boss will understand.'

'No, it's okay,' I say. 'You go to work.'

'Well, let me know if you need anything. I can write down my work number if you need it.'

'No, it's okay. I can look it up.'

He leaves. I delete my unread email notifications and take a photo of me in my hospital gown looking as sick as possible and send it to my ex-girlfriend, then I turn my phone off. I try to read the book but my eyes can't focus on the words. I go back to sleep.

The nurse wakes me up and changes my drip and tells me a doctor will be in soon. She leaves then the doctor comes in.

The doctor introduces himself but I forget his name as soon as he says it. He holds his clipboard above his chest where his name badge is. 'The blood test has come back and it's what we thought it was. Have you heard of serotonin syndrome?'

'Yes,' I say. 'What do we do now?'

'We're going to flush your medication out of your system. You might get a bit sad.'

'I'm already a bit sad,' I say.

'Yes, well that will probably get worse tomorrow, but then you can go back on your antidepressants and you'll be right as rain.'

'Thanks.'

The doctor leaves. I look at the curtains and can see a shadow on the other side of someone sitting up in bed.

A new psychiatrist comes in and introduces himself. I make a decision to stop trying to remember anyone's name. He asks how I'm feeling and before I have time to answer he gives me a benzo to deal with the withdrawal symptoms I'll soon be feeling.

Lunch arrives and the psychiatrist says, 'I'll leave you to eat lunch.'

For lunch there is a ham sandwich with cheese and lettuce. To drink, a plastic cup of orange juice and for lunch dessert, custard. I am a vegetarian. I don't remember if I have told anyone this.

'Excuse me,' I say to a nurse walking past. 'Sorry. I got a ham sandwich, but I am vegetarian'.

'Oh, that's no problem,' the nurse says. She takes my ham sandwich and throws it in a bin.

The shadow in the bed next to me hears this and complains that he didn't get a ham sandwich. His only has cheese and lettuce in it. The nurse apologises and takes his sandwich and also throws it in the bin.

'I'll be right back with new sandwiches for both of you,' the nurse says.

I eat the custard and drink the orange juice and wait for my new sandwich.

While I'm waiting, my ex-girlfriend storms into the ward holding flowers and a box of juice, with a shopping bag hanging from her elbow. I quickly pick up my book before she sees me.

She arrives at my bed and says, 'What the fuck.' She has had a haircut and it looks good.

I slowly put down my book and look up at her. 'What,' I say in a voice croakier than it needs to be.

'You can't just send someone a photo of you in hospital and then not answer your phone,' she says.

'My phone ran out of battery,' I say.

She puts the flowers in my jug of water, then rips off the purple transparent paper so I can see the flowers properly from my bed. 'Still. You can't do that.'

'Sorry.'

'You're not here, because, you know, are you?'

'I don't know,' I say, even though I do.

'It wasn't because of me and how I, you know?'

'No, I didn't try to kill myself because you broke up with me.'

'Good. That would be a really shitty thing to do.'

'Yeah, I know, that's why I didn't do it.' I forget to put on my croaky voice so I fake cough, then I cough for real then I can't stop coughing.

She sits on the side of the bed next to me even though there is a chair right next to it. 'Sorry. I'm just glad you're okay.'

'Well, I'm not really okay, I'm in hospital,' I say.

The nurse comes back with my sandwich. She sees the flowers and says, 'You can't put those in there. You have to bring your own vase.' She takes the flowers out of the water jug and places them flat on the table facing away from me, then she takes the water jug away.

I give my ex-girlfriend my water bottle to put the flowers in, but it is too top-heavy and falls over. She grabs the flowers and water spills onto the floor.

'I'll go and get you a vase,' my ex-girlfriend says.

'No, don't bother, it's okay,' I say.

'Well, what should I do – nothing? Should I just let the flowers die?'

'They'll be fine for now.'

'So what's wrong with you? Why are you here?'

'Something to do with my antidepressants, they're poisoning me or something. Some sort of overdose.'

'So you did, then?'

'No.'

'Well, if it was because of me, I'm sorry.'

'Don't be sorry. Just don't do it again,' I say. She looks at me and I regret saying it.

'What is that supposed to mean?'

'Nothing, it was just a joke.'

'Oh, fuck off.'

'Sorry.'

'This is so you,' she says. 'You're always talking about how sad you are, but then you never act on it. You're always making dumb jokes instead of feeling anything.'

'Yeah, I know.'

'You're not allowed to respond with "okay" after someone breaks up with you. You need to actually feel something.'

'Yeah, I know.'

'You're always talking about how sad you are and you make me cry. Do your own feeling.' She pulls a bag of apples and a bag of lollies out of the plastic bag. 'I got you these, I know the food is terrible here.'

'The food is fine.'

The nurse returns with the water jug filled up and pours me a glass of water.

'Is everything all right here?' she asks.

'Yeah, we're fine,' I say.

'Sorry,' my ex-girlfriend says to the nurse. 'Sorry,' my ex-girlfriend says to me.

'It's not your fault,' I say. 'It's nothing. It's just an accident or something that happened. It's no one's fault.'

'No. I mean I'm sorry for what I said just now.'

'Why is there water all over the floor?' says the nurse.

'I probably deserved it,' I say to my ex-girlfriend.

'Yeah, well, there's a time and a place, right?'

'I'll send somebody to clean this up,' the nurse says, and leaves.

'I guess I'm sorry too,' I say.

'What have you been doing lately?' she asks. 'Since the other week?'

'Writing. I have decided I want to take it seriously so I'm writing every day.'

'That's good to hear,' she says. 'It's nice to know you're doing okay.'

'But then my computer broke which kind of ruined everything,' I say.

'Are you getting it fixed?'

'Yeah. I was meant to pick it up today,' I say. 'What have you been doing?'

'Crying,' she says.

'Sorry,' I say.

'No. It's okay. Crying is good,' she says. She touches my leg.

'You also got a haircut,' I say.

She looks at me and smiles. 'Yeah, I did.'

'Was the hairdresser weird about you crying the whole time?'

'Yeah, it was a bit awkward.' She laughs and then pats my leg. 'I'm going to go get you a vase. I'll be right back.'

When she leaves I get out of bed and go to the toilet. I wheel the pole attached to the bag of fluid, attached to the tube, attached to me. After I pee I take some paper hand towels back to my bed to soak up the spilled water. I put them on the water and push them around with my feet. They soak up most of it, but leave some streaks on the linoleum. Instead of picking them up I kick them under the bed.

I rip the rest of the paper off the flowers and lean them against the water jug. I eat my sandwich slowly so that when my ex-girlfriend comes back I can finish it in front of her to make it look like I was doing something more than just waiting for her. It takes five minutes to eat the first half of the sandwich, ten minutes to eat half of the remaining half and after half an hour I accept that she isn't coming back so

I finish the sandwich.

I sleep for a while and wake up when my flatmate returns with my phone charger. He's in a rush because his sister is waiting in the carpark. 'She sends her love,' he tells me. I say thanks and plug in my phone. I turn on my phone and see I have several missed calls from my ex-girlfriend and half a dozen texts. The latest one says 'Hey. I went to buy a vase but the cheapest one was $40 so I freaked out and left. Sorry. Text me when you're out. xox.'

I try to call my dad. He doesn't answer. He never carries his phone around with him. I try to remember the home phone number but can't and it's not in my contacts. I text him, 'I'm in hospital. I'm fine. Will be out tomorrow.'

My phone rings. I recognise the number as the computer shop. I told them I would collect my computer today and it is now after 5pm. I don't answer, but I also don't cancel the call so it looks like I just missed it. A nurse tells me to put my phone on silent. I turn my phone off. I have a headache. I tell the nurse and she gives me paracetamol. The headache doesn't go away.

For dinner I am given a mound of rice, green beans and two vegetarian sausages with no tomato sauce. To drink, a plastic cup of orange juice and for dessert, rice pudding with dates in it. The food is fine. I read my book for a bit and then go to sleep.

In the middle of the night I am woken up by the man next to me yelling. 'Nurse. Help. Help.'

A nurse comes and turns the light on. The curtain has been pulled back sometime in the night and I can see him. The head of his bed is elevated and he has fallen down in a heap at the foot.

'Help me. Help me,' he keeps yelling.

The nurse makes soothing shushing sounds and pulls the curtain between our beds shut. 'Just wiggle your bottom. Wiggle your bottom and I'll pull you up the bed. Just keep wiggling your bottom. Come on, move with me, move with me,' the nurse says.

I play Sudoku on my phone. The nurse pokes her head through the curtain as she passes and tells me to go to sleep.

For breakfast I am given a small bowl of rice bubbles, a banana, two pieces of cheap white toast, butter in a small plastic container with a foil tearaway lid, and strawberry jam in a plastic container with a foil tearaway lid. To drink, a glass of orange juice. There is no dessert, even though the piece of paper says fruit salad.

A nurse comes and changes my drip. She checks my temperature. 'It's almost back to normal. You should be discharged this afternoon,' she says.

'Thank you.'

I text my flatmate and ask him to bring me my shoes. He doesn't reply.

A psychiatrist comes around. 'I'm here to make sure you will be fine after you're discharged. I see you accidentally double-dosed your antidepressants.'

'I don't think I did.'

'Well, that's what your forms say.'

'I don't think I did though.'

'Well, you signed the form saying you did.'

'Okay, maybe I did then,' I say. I don't think I did.

'Okay, so for the time being we're lowering your dose to seventy-five milligrams for the next two days, then back up to one hundred and fifty milligrams after. We have talked to your GP and she said she will call you tomorrow to arrange a meeting next week where you can discuss your medication further.'

'Okay.'

'She has also expressed concern over your mental health. Because this wasn't intentional we are not going to refer you to our community care team, but if you feel like you need more support she is happy to refer you.'

'Thank you.'

'And I also wanted to check, if you needed them, that you have the numbers for the emergency crisis team.'

'Yes. I have them.'

'Okay, well I have this pamphlet here that you can take home with you. And on the back there are numbers you can call if you need to.'

'Thanks. I already have them but thanks.'

'Well, I'll leave this with you anyway. So the main thing I'm doing here is I'm making sure you know how much your dose is.'

'Yes, I know what it is.'

'Here's a script for a week, with a repeat for next week. That should get you through until you see your doctor. Now that's one capsule tonight, one capsule tomorrow night, then two at night from then on.'

'Yes, I know.'

'And if you miss a dose, and it's been longer than twelve hours, don't take any extra. Just wait until you would next normally take it and take your normal dose.'

'Yes, I know.'

'We're just making sure you don't have any more accidents and end up back here.'

'Thank you. I know. I'm fine.'

I check my emails and there are several emails from my

boss asking where I am and why I was not at work today. I send him an email saying, 'Sorry I wasn't at work today. I am in the hospital.' I attach the same photo I sent to my ex-girlfriend earlier.

My phone vibrates. It's a call from my dad.

'Sorry I didn't see this sooner,' he says. 'I only just cleared my messages.'

'It's okay, it's not a big deal. I'll be getting discharged in a few hours.'

'You didn't . . . did you?'

'No, I didn't do anything.'

'Because I know you sometimes feel down.'

'Yes. I didn't. Don't worry.'

'Well if you did, that's okay. We're here to help.'

'I didn't but thank you.'

'Have you told your mother?'

'Yeah,' I say. 'I was just talking to her now.' I wasn't. I have decided to wait until I am out of hospital to tell her, because otherwise she will book a flight to be here as soon as she can.

'That's good to hear.'

'Also, I need to borrow some money. My computer is broken and I have to pay for it to be fixed.'

'Okay. Things are a bit tight here at the moment.'

'It's just. My work is only giving me part-time hours at the moment.'

'I understand that.'

'And I don't think I have any sick leave yet. So I need to use all my savings to pay rent for this week since I'm not working.'

'I suppose you're right. I'll transfer some money from the house account and get back to you later.'

'Thanks Dad. I need to go. I'll call you when I'm discharged.'

'You know I love you right?' Dad says. He's started saying

this at the end of every phone call.

'Yes I know,' I say.

A nurse checks my temperature. 'It's looking good. We'll just let this drip empty, then you can probably go home.'

I text my flatmate again and ask him to bring me my shoes. He doesn't reply.

For lunch I'm given a bread roll, three pieces of cheese, a plastic container of butter with a tearaway foil lid, and a small bowl of pumpkin soup. To drink, a plastic cup of orange juice, and for dessert, peaches and cream.

The drip empties and a nurse disconnects the tube from my arm, then pulls out the needle and tapes a piece of cotton wool over the needle mark.

A doctor arrives. 'Everything seems to be good. You know the changes to your medication over the next week?'

'Yes, the psychiatrist told me.'

'Good. It's one 75-milligram capsule tonight, and tomorrow, and two from then on.'

'Yes, the psychiatrist told me.'

'Great, you're all ready to go then.'

He leaves. The nurse leaves. I stack my phone, charger, book and juice on my bedside table and sit upright on my bed. I wait.

Quarter of an hour later, the nurse arrives. 'I thought you were discharged?'

'I was told I'm ready to go, but no one told me what to do.'

She looks at her clipboard. 'Oh yes, you need to sign out.' She disappears behind the curtain and reappears with another clipboard. 'Sign this. Do you have someone picking you up?'

'I'm waiting for my shoes to arrive so I can walk home.'

'If you don't have anyone picking you up, we can call a taxi.'

'I'll walk home. I just need my shoes.'

'Okay, well, we need this bed, so would you be okay waiting in the ED waiting room?'

'Okay, I'll just get changed.'

She leaves. I climb out of bed and pull on my shorts and T-shirt. They're still damp. I am not sure if they smell bad, or if it's me that smells bad. I pull back the curtain and look for the nurse. I can't see her. I pack the bag of apples and the box of juice, neither of which I've touched, into the plastic bag my ex-girlfriend brought. I've eaten all the lollies so I leave the empty packet on the bedside table. I put my book in the bag and start to leave, but then I remember my phone charger so return to get it and put it in the bag. I hold the flowers in my other hand. I follow the EXIT sign down a hallway and around the corner and find a door that leads outside near the ED waiting room. I walk out the door and then back inside through the ED entrance.

I text my flatmate, 'I've just been discharged and need my shoes. Waiting in ED.'

He texts back, 'I'll be there in twenty minutes.'

I text my dad, 'Discharged. Am tired. Will call tomorrow.'

My flatmate arrives with my shoes. I put them on. I don't have any socks. We walk home. It only takes ten minutes but by the time I get through the door I am exhausted. I put the flowers in a coffee plunger full of water and put them on the table. I take the book out of the shopping bag and put the bag in the fridge.

I text my ex-girlfriend and tell her I'm out of hospital.

'Do you want me to come over?' she responds.

'Okay.'

I have a long shower and clean myself three times over with soap. I wash and condition my hair and spend a long time thoroughly patting down every part of my body with a towel.

I put on deodorant and cover my face with shaving cream, but as I hold my razor up to my face I notice I'm shaking so I wash off the shaving cream without shaving so I don't cut myself. I use the moisturiser my ex-girlfriend gave me on my face and arms and rub the excess into my chest. I get changed into clean clothes.

My ex-girlfriend arrives. 'You look good,' she says. 'Better.'

'Thanks.'

'Do you feel better?'

'Yeah. Much better.'

She puts her tote bag on the table and pulls my laptop out of it. 'I picked this up for you,' she says.

I don't know what to say. She looks at me and smiles. 'I'll pay you back,' I say. 'Dad is giving me money.'

'Yeah. Of course,' she says. 'I mean I wasn't going to pay for it.'

'Yeah. I was going to pick it up tomorrow but this is much better.'

I look down at my feet and then she says, 'What do you want for dinner? We can go to the supermarket, and I'll make anything. You must be sick of that hospital food.'

'The food was fine.'

'Okay, whatever you say. What do you want?'

'I don't want you to feel like you have to cook for me,' I say.

She looks at me and then says, 'Okay, what do you want to do.'

We order curry from the Indian place down the road. We wait fifteen minutes before walking down to get it. The sun is on the horizon and the air outside feels a lot cooler on my skin than it did when I left the hospital. I wish I had another layer on. I pay for both curries. The short walk back home takes all the energy I have.

While we are eating, she looks at the flowers in the plunger on the table and touches my hand. 'You brought them home,' she says.

'Yeah. I wasn't going to leave them there,' I say.

She rubs my knuckles. 'I like that you moisturise,' she says.

'What?'

'You're not the hottest guy in the world, but at least you moisturise.'

'Yeah, well you bought it for me.'

'Do you want to watch a movie or something?' she asks after we finish eating.

'No, I'm pretty tired, I think I'm gonna go to bed,' I say.

'Do you want me to stay over?'

'No. I'm fine.'

She starts packing up her things and I say goodbye and take my laptop to my room and shut the door. All the windows I opened days ago are still open. I'm annoyed at my flatmate for not closing them while I was in hospital. I close the windows. My room is cold. I look at the duvet, sheets and pillows piled in the middle of the room and decide to sleep in my sleeping bag. I take it out of my wardrobe and crawl in. I turn on my laptop. It takes a little while to start up and I get worried for a short time, but once it is up and running it is all right.

I see Kanye West has released a new music video. It's lo-fi and is directed by Spike Jonze and looks like it is filmed on an iPhone. It starts with Kanye West running down an empty broken road in the rain and he's laughing. The laughter is slowed down and sounds disturbing. He sings along to the song, but mumbles some of the words. He's holding the hand of his daughter North West. She touches his leg. He holds her and they're standing in the rain and both wearing very good clothes. Kanye pulls North West's hood up so she is protected from the rain, and I cry.

I watch the video again and continue crying. I take my phone out and film myself crying and send the video to my ex-girlfriend.

I watch the video I have just sent. I'm smiling and it isn't clear whether I'm crying or laughing until the tears start leaving shiny lines on my cheeks and the corners of my mouth fall. I look directly into the camera and wipe my nose on my wrist and you can see snot in my nostrils. I splutter and Kanye sings, 'Hello my only one.' The lyrics are nostalgic and romantic. Even though Kanye's voice is auto-tuned, he sounds very genuine.

I text my ex-girlfriend, 'Don't read anything into the lyrics.' I see my phone is on 4 percent battery. I reach down next to my bed to plug it in, but my charger is not there. I wonder if I left it at the hospital, but I remember putting it in the plastic bag, which is now in the fridge. I turn my phone off and throw it into the pile of bedding.

MY FRIEND ROD

My friend Rod is convinced I don't like him. He thinks that because he's loud and I'm quiet, and he's touchy and I'm not, that I have something against him. I don't. Everyone likes Rod; he's fun and he knows how to have a good time. When we're out drinking, and Holly says, 'Let's invite Rod,' everyone screams, 'Yaaaas, I love Rod.' I say, 'Yes, we all love Rod,' but I don't scream it, but that isn't because I don't like Rod; it's because I'm not the type of person who screams.

If you text Rod, he'll come. He'll rock up with his finger guns and his V-neck T-shirt, and everyone except me will go crazy. Again, it's not because I don't like Rod; it's because it takes more than someone arriving to make me go crazy. Tyler is my best friend and I never go crazy when he arrives. I just look up and say, 'Hey Tyler,' and that's enough.

No one is quite sure where Rod came from. He went to school with Stephen, but when asked, Stephen says, 'Yeah, technically he was there, but he never showed up and I didn't really become friends with him until Sasha started inviting him round.' Sasha said that he was friends with Tyler first, and Tyler said he was friends with Jeremy. Jeremy said that he only became good friends with Rod through Sasha. Holly is usually the one to text him these days, but she was probably the last person to get to know him because she only came back from London a couple of months ago.

But I can't ask 'Where did you come from Rod?' because 'Where did you come from?' really means 'Why are you here?' which really means 'Why don't you go back to where you're from?' And it's not that I want Rod to go back to where he came from; I am just curious about where that actually is. I want to know why someone so universally loved is never too busy to party. Where are all his other friends?

Rod walks in like he's dancing, with little steps this way and that, and an unnecessary amount of hip movement. The table erupts with arms and bodies and drinks slosh around, spilling out of their glasses. I raise my glass sensibly towards him and nod.

'What have you been up to tonight?' Sasha asks Rod.

'Was just at a party, but it was kind of dying.'

I don't believe it. No party with Rod in attendance could possibly be dying. Rod is the party. He's fun and he knows how to have a good time. But there's no time to question him because now that he has arrived, the party can begin. He orders a round of shots and soon everyone's on the dance floor. I stay at our seats and guard the bags.

Occasionally between songs Tyler or Holly will come and sit down and we'll have a good nice chat, and other times I'm happy to just sit by myself and watch. I'm not having a bad time; I'm just not a dancer. After a while Rod comes up to me and says, 'I know you don't like me much,' and I have to reassure him that I do, in fact, like him.

'Of course I like you Rod,' I say to Rod. 'Everyone likes you. You're fun and you know how to have a good time.'

But to be honest, he's right; I don't like Rod and I do want him to go back where he came from. He's loud and always touching me. He yells and is always drunk. He's always sneaking up behind me and zapping my waist and laughing. We get it, Rod, you're fun, you know how to have a good time! But there's no point in him knowing I don't like him. All my friends like him, so I put up with him. That's just part of being a good friend.

I offer to buy Rod a pint, but he wants a Corona, even though it's not as nice and is worse value for money. But he insists because he just wants something 'refreshing'. I order a pale ale for myself and a Corona for Rod, and before I've even finished paying for it he's taken it and returned to the dance floor. He pushes his slice of lemon into his disgusting beer and is back at the centre of attention. He's got his arms in the air and his feet going, and he spins around and yells and everyone else yells too.

I see what people like about Rod. He's fun. He's handsome in an over-the-top way. He knows how to have a good time. These are good qualities, but they're not qualities I value. It's not that I dislike people who know how to have a good time; I just don't care if someone knows how to have a good time. Put it this way: if you disliked someone because they didn't know how to have a good time, that would be cruel.

We move from bar to bar, dancing our way from one side of town to the other. Rod picks up a group of people with a conga line, who follow us to the next bar. I do a bit of dancing here and there, and I chat to whoever is tired of dancing. I guess this is what clubbing is. It's not my thing, but I play along.

After another three or four bars, people start dropping off, going home either in pairs or alone. We spill out of the final club – a concrete bunker with a disco ball and flashing lights –

and onto the street. Tyler and Sasha disappear into a crowded burger joint, and Rod, Holly and I walk together back down the main drag. Just as I'm about to pack it in and go home, Rod stops outside the karaoke club.

'Just one song,' he says.

Holly shrugs and we follow him inside.

The club is dark with red velvet everywhere. Bright lights shine in blue and white onto the stage, where a man is singing 'I'm Gonna Be (500 Miles)' by the Proclaimers and marching on the spot. Rod immediately signs up and says to us, 'Okay, which one of you is ready to have the time of your life?' Holly refuses, and Rod turns to me.

'Come on. I'll even be the girl,' he says.

I agree because I am also fun and I also know how to have a good time. Holly smiles. Rod buys us a round of Coronas that come in a bucket filled with ice, and we find a table near the stage to wait our turn. Each of the other tables seem to have their own Rod, singing along with their entire body and eagerly awaiting their turn for karaoke.

Our turn comes, and Rod and I abandon our drinks and get on stage. '(I've Had) the Time of My Life' is queued. The first frame of the music video is frozen on a small screen at the front and centre of the stage, with the song title in a cartoonish font plastered on top. The same image is projected behind us. After nodding to the DJ that we're ready, the song starts. The lyrics come in sooner than I expect, and I stumble with the first line and focus on catching up rather than getting the melody right. Rod nails his first line; he sings in falsetto and doesn't have to look at the screen, instead looking out at the audience with his arms opened wide. The funky bass comes in and Rod starts swinging his hips towards me. I take a step back, out of the main lights and into the shadow at the side of the stage. I manage to catch the next round of lyrics in time, and by the time 'This could be love' comes in, I've got the croon down. I can hear people in the crowd singing along to the chorus. I take a step forward, back into the light. I look out into the crowd, but between the lights in my eyes and the dark room, they're invisible. Rod bangs his finger guns at me and I jut my shoulder back like I've been shot. We smile at each other. During the saxophone solo, I take another step forward and look out into the blackness and hold my arm up into the light. Blue light catches my fingers and I curl them into a fist. My eyes get used to the darkness and I look in Holly's direction and make out her face beaming up at us. I bend my elbow and bring my fist down in victory. Meanwhile, Rod is thrusting his hips back and forth sexually. We turn to each other for the final chorus; he points at me, sings the final 'owe it all to you', drops his microphone, takes a couple of steps back. I shake my head but there's no stopping him. He runs towards me and leaps, and I catch him. I try lifting him into the air but we fall to the floor. Rod gets up instantly and pulls me to my feet. We leave the stage to applause and I start to see Rod's appeal.

Holly greets us with a hug at the bottom of the stairs.

'You were amazing,' she says to both of us, then turns to me specifically, and says, 'I had no idea you had it in you.'

She leans into me and bunches the back of my T-shirt in her fist. We return to the table and I finish off the last of my Corona. It's tasteless but cold and refreshing. I say to Holly, because she lives just down the road from me, 'Hey, do you want to split a taxi home?'

Holly looks at me, then Holly looks at Rod, and Rod raises his eyebrows, and Holly says, 'No, you go ahead, I think I'm going to stick around a while longer.' And I get it. Rod is fun, and Rod knows how to have a good time. I get it.

JOBS

I've got one job in an office for twenty hours a week, four hours each day in the mornings. That covers my rent, bills and groceries. The job started with me doing basic admin, things like scheduling meetings and replying to emails for my boss, but recently they have started asking me to write copy and press releases and sit in on marketing meetings because they say I'm good with words. I'm still quite slow and make a lot of mistakes but hopefully soon I will be able to move into that type of work all the time.

Sometimes when I'm at the office, everyone else just leaves and it's expected that I will be able to stay and man the phones and close up. It's okay because it gives me time in lieu. When no one else is there and the phone rings I usually let it go to the answering machine. I can't really help anyone who calls anyway. If anyone asks I can say I was in the toilet, but no one ever has. The second time the phone rings I always answer. It would be possible to take two toilet breaks over a couple of hours, but it would be a pretty massive coincidence for the phone to ring during both of them. At five o'clock the air conditioning turns off, and everything goes silent in a way that makes me uncomfortable and I leave as fast as possible.

At my job I wear collared shirts, which I keep hanging in one of my wardrobes. My room has two wardrobes. I got the biggest room in my flat because I was the only one with a stable job when we moved in. None of the other rooms have any wardrobes. I only use one of the wardrobes and let my flatmates use the other one. I was never told that I had to wear shirts, but everyone else in the office wears them so I do too. I only own five shirts, but I make sure to mix them up and not wear the same shirt on the same day of the week two weeks in a row. I have a dozen T-shirts and only two days to wear them.

There was a pimple on the back of my neck a few months ago. I squeezed it every morning, and it never went away. It's still there but it's now more of a scab. I try to leave it alone but I always end up picking at it during stressful moments. I've got a small brown dot inside all my collars. I have a second job at a café on Saturdays and a couple of afternoons a week. That covers my spending money. There's an alleyway lined by tall buildings between my jobs where at midday the sun shines onto one building's glass facade, reflects onto another building's glass facade, and illuminates a third building's glass facade. I always take a moment to look up at the shining buildings and appreciate how it looks like every illustration I have ever seen of a utopia. I've been working at this café for a couple of years now and if I could just get a few more hours at my office job I would be able to leave.

I've got a third job. It's for a friend who started a shop that sells vegan snacks and upcycled fashion and small handmade pieces of jewellery. I met her through a vegan club and she offered me a job because I was vegan and needed the money. Now I work there more as a favour to her whenever it's busy and she needs someone to cover or when her regular staff go on holiday. I am reliable and know my way around the point of sale system. She usually lets me know far enough in advance that I can request leave to use my time in lieu from my office job. The money from the vegan job goes straight into savings.

On the afternoons I'm not working at the café I come home and try to spend a good few hours writing. When I get home I usually spend an hour talking to a flatmate before excusing myself to my room to write and then it takes about an hour to get myself in the zone, and then I only get about an hour of writing done. I'm trying to treat it more like a job. I don't make a lot of money from it, but occasionally I'll get a gig that pays a couple of hundred dollars. With that money I buy myself something unnecessary and nice.

I'm looking after myself now. I floss. I wash my sheets every two weeks. I drink, but not to excess. I meditate. I get eight hours' sleep and wake up early. I read for forty-five minutes every night before sleeping but I don't read in bed because of sleep hygiene. I do half an hour of cardio, usually a run, every evening three to four hours before I go to sleep. I bought a watch that counts my steps and measures my heart rate. I get ten thousand steps every day and have not missed a day for over six months.

I was doing ten push-ups a day until I read on the internet that the only thing ten push-ups a day gets you good at is ten push-ups a day. So I pushed myself to up my daily target each week. I've now settled on twenty-five push-ups, three times a day. Once when I wake up, once when I get home and once about an hour before I go to sleep. Sometimes I do as many push-ups as I possibly can before I collapse so I can see how much I've progressed.

I used to do burpees and squats, but the burpees made the liquor cabinet in the hallway shake and after a month of squats my already substantial thighs had beefed up and could no longer fit in my jeans. Once I planked for thirty or forty seconds but it felt like a waste of time.

I want to build muscle and lose fat. It's hard to do high protein and low carb when you're vegetarian so, for the first time in years, I am eating meat again. I'm in a privileged enough position that I can afford to buy organic free-range chicken, so I feel like I have an obligation to. I haven't told my friend who runs the vegan store that I'm eating meat again. I cook most nights. As far as milk goes I usually drink soy. Except sometimes I drink a glass of regular milk and remember how my ex-girlfriend's breath always used to smell like milk.

I've been putting myself out there. Going on dates with girls I meet online. We sit across from each other and go through the same conversation about what we are doing with our lives. I list all the things I'm doing and they say, 'Wow, you're busy.'

And I say, 'Yeah, I guess I am.'

And sometimes they ask, 'Are you too busy for a relationship?'

I say, 'No, I would make time if I met the right person.' The dates usually end shortly after that.

I made enough time for my ex, but then she said she didn't think I liked her enough to continue the relationship and that I wasn't into her, just that I wanted someone, but I liked her more than I have ever liked anyone and if that wasn't enough I'm not even sure if I have what it takes to like anyone.

I've been working on improving all the things she said were wrong with me. She said I had no structure to my life and now I have a strict routine. She said I couldn't feel anything so I have been working on my feelings and expressing them appropriately. I listen to others and try to relate to what they are saying, but not talk over them. I know how to communicate in a healthy way and have been complimented on my openness.

I was seeing a counsellor until six months ago, when I was told that I no longer met the criteria for funded sessions because I was earning too much money and was not in a critical enough state. My counsellor gave me a burned CD of guided meditations which he said I should listen to every day, except when I'm busy, when I should listen to them twice. I listen to them when I'm on my run and pay attention to how my breath speeds up as I go up hills and the feeling of my feet in the bottoms of my shoes.

On every date I go on, I look at the girl and have a bad thought that this girl is not as interesting or as good-looking as my ex. When I was dating her I was fatter and poorer and my life was a mess, and now I am fit and healthy and stable, both emotionally and financially. Surely I should be doing better romantically now. This is something I am not open about.

I carry on doing all the right things, I reply to every photo they send me with heart eyes emojis, I tell them when I'm going to be busy so they don't wonder why I'm not replying to their messages. I never cancel dates, and I look in their eyes before I kiss them.

I have made a decision to avoid dating girls who look like my ex. So no girls who are medium-skinny and medium-short with medium-brown medium-length hair with either a fringe or not because she grew it out while we were dating but as soon as we broke up she cut it back to the way it was when I first met her. I would hate to bump into her on the street if I was with a new girlfriend who looks like her. It wasn't until I made this rule that I realised almost all girls look like that.

The last time I contacted my ex was when I sent her an email with a story I had written which I was entering into a competition. 'It's fiction,' I wrote in the body of the email. I always contact her by email. I have her phone number and we are still friends on several other websites, but email seems like the most detached option.

'You just wrote down something that happened to us,' she wrote back.

'When it happened to us it was non-fiction,' I said, 'but when I wrote it in the story it's fiction.'

'Can you at least change my name?'

'It's not you, it's a fictional character with the same name as you.'

I tried to think of a new name for the character, but nothing quite fit, so I changed it so the character was referred to as 'my ex-girlfriend' and then I changed details of the story to make the ex-girlfriend character nicer.

I recently bought my first pair of blue jeans since I was a child. I felt like it was a significant metaphorical change. I was leaving behind my depression-tinged teenage black jeans and embracing an everyman aesthetic. I thought this would warrant comments, but no one has mentioned them. I guess I have been the type of person who would wear blue jeans for quite a few years now, and I have only just caught up. They are not skinny jeans, but are tight around my thighs. I used to be self-conscious about my thighs until my ex told me they were her favourite part of my body. Her hands would often find their way to them when we were in bed or on a couch together. She also said she liked the hair on my lower back, which she used to rub between her fingers, making tiny dreadlocks. Since breaking up my legs have only gotten stronger and my back has gotten hairier but no girl has gravitated towards either of them.

I am being more conscious about my money. I went down to the next lowest phone plan. It saves me $10 a month. All I need to do is be more mindful of data usage. When I'm low on minutes I call Dad and hang up before he answers, so it looks like he has a missed call, and he calls me back. I know when buses move from on-peak to off-peak and plan my trips accordingly. I stock up on foods when they're on special. I've got at least a week's supply of chicken breasts in my freezer and a stack of extra cans in my wardrobe.

I talk to Mum every week. She asks me how my jobs are going and I say good, and she asks how my writing is going and I say I've written some new stories and have sent them in to some competitions. She asks if I need money and I say I don't and she asks if I've seen Toby recently and I say I haven't but we have plans to catch up.

Whenever I talk to Dad he tells me I should go back to school. He says I should get some real hard skills that will keep me employed for longer. I tell him, 'I'm doing fine and things are getting better and better for me. I'm stable and employed and have paid off most of my debts.'

'But that could all change any day,' he says. 'You need security.'

'Everyone I know has jobs like this,' I say.

'It's because everyone you know went to university to study sociology,' he says.

That's not true. None of my friends studied sociology, but I know a lot who majored in art history and anthropology, so I let it slide.

I have been going to potlucks organised by the local vegan club. I signed up for the newsletter years ago and never got around to unsubscribing when I stopped being vegan. I always used to ignore the invites because the only people who go to potlucks are people whose only interests are going to potlucks, but I met a girl who was going, so I went too. I made falafel which was too dry and fell apart when you picked it up. People crumbled it on top of salads and casseroles and told me it was delicious. I keep going back to the potlucks, even though I have lost interest in the girl. I have learned how to make falafel stick together using chia seeds. The people at the potlucks are not only interested in potlucks. They are also interested in sustainability and cycling and tramping. They told me about how the air feels different when you have climbed high up and that it is exciting to walk eight hours for no reason other than that you are going to turn around and walk back again the next day. So I bought a pair of tramping boots.

I called in sick to my job and we drove out of the city for three hours and pulled into a bay on the side of the road. We walked into the bush on a gradual incline and then a decline down towards a river. After an hour and a half my watch buzzed, telling me I had walked ten thousand steps, and we kept walking. After two hours I started to feel my bag's weight on my shoulders. My bag is not very big. All it had in it was a sleeping bag and a change of clothes. I should have bought a bag with wider shoulder straps and a clip around my torso, but I didn't want to buy a new one just for this trip. Everything else I needed was being carried by my strongest new friend, Dan. He was carrying all our food and water, a pack of cards, a set of dominos, three books, a coil of rope, and a bottle of whisky to share. He packed his bag tight and dense. He rolled up all his clothes and made room for a first-aid kit.

We stopped for a break and Dan took an entire fruit cake out of his bag and cut it up with a pocket knife. We spread margarine from a Ziploc bag on the cake and sat in the dry riverbed. Dan asked if we wanted another slice, and we said that we should save it for the next day and he said he had another one in his bag for tomorrow so we ate the rest of the cake. Dan disappeared back into the bush for a wee and his girlfriend Jane found a boulder the same size as the fruitcake and hid it in his bag under a raincoat.

We looked at the sky and the time and decided to take a detour on the way to the hut. The detour took us over the top of a peak and added another four hours to our four-hour walk, and we did it because we wanted to. We climbed and climbed until the bush disappeared, and we kept climbing. The path curled around the hill and then back again, avoiding the steep cliffs. The battery in my watch died. The air got cool and we stopped to drink water from Dan's backpack, then we climbed some more. We got to the top, and there was a sheer cliff face down to the riverbed below. I looked up at the sky. I expected it to look bigger and brighter but it looked exactly the same as it usually does. But I spent some time looking at it and it did look beautiful. I stood right at the edge of the cliff, looking down, kicking stones and watching them fall, creating puffs of dust as they bounced off the face on their way down, and no one was scared.

ACKNOWLEDGEMENTS

'Debts' was first published in *Kill Your Darlings*; 'Santa the Christmas Hedgehog' was first published in *Turbine | Kapohau*; 'Three Pizzas' and 'Dog Farm, Food Game' were first published in *Sport*; and 'My Friend Rod' was broadcast on RNZ. I would like to thank the editors of these publications.

I would like to thank Freya Daly Sadgrove for being there at every stage of this book. Thanks to David Klein who has taught me so much about how to be a person. And kind regards to my long time colleague Alice May Connolly whose ongoing presence has been noted.

Thanks Pip Adam and Emily Perkins for being both the most supportive and encouraging supervisors I could ask for, and also for reminding me that it was important for my work to be good. Thanks to my MA Class for an amazing year and all the ongoing support since 2016. Thanks to William Brandt for giving me feedback that was essential to the shaping of the book. Thanks to my other creative writing teachers over the years: Jessie Hennen, Dave Armstrong, Kate Duignan and Patrick Evans.

Thanks to everyone at VUP, especially Ashleigh and Fergus.

Thanks to Ruby Urquhart for the artwork and Ebony Lamb for the photos.

Thanks to this long list of friends whose support has been essential in getting me and this book to the stage it is in: Annaleese Jochems, Ox Lennon, Eddie Crawshaw, Jake Brown, Callum Devlin, Oliver Devlin, Eleanor Rose King Merton, Jamie Penwarden, Jackson Nieuwland, Carolyn DeCarlo, Kezia Fairbrother, Jono Edwards, Rose Lu, Jonny Potts, Adam Goodall, Hannah Griffin, Ruby Cumming, Tom White, Demi Heath, Gerv Lawrie, Holly Hunter, Naomi Arnold, Hera Lindsay Bird, Moe Zass and Uther Dean.

Thanks to all the comedy, theatre and writing festivals, venues, producers, artists and audiences over the years. For some reason there is an idea that writing is a solitary act. It is not. Without these communities I would not be anywhere.

Finally thanks to all my family and especially to Mum, Dad and Karen and my siblings Paul, Jamie, Rebecca, Shaun and Ashleigh.